White Collared
Part One: Mercy

Jenn –

Enjoy !

Shelly
Bell

By Shelly Bell

White Collared Part One: Mercy

SHELLY BELL

AVON
IMPULSE
An Imprint of HarperCollins Publishers

This is a work of fiction. Names, characters, places, and incidents are products of the author's imagination or are used fictitiously and are not to be construed as real. Any resemblance to actual events, locales, organizations, or persons, living or dead, is entirely coincidental.

Excerpt from *Catching Cameron* copyright © 2014 by Julie Revell Benjamin.
Excerpt from *Daring Miss Danvers* copyright © 2014 by Vivienne Lorret.
Excerpt from *Woo'd in Haste* copyright © 2014 by Sabrina Darby.
Excerpt from *Bad Girls Don't Marry Marines* copyright © 2014 by Codi Gary.
Excerpt from *Various States of Undress: Carolina* copyright © 2014 by Laura Simcox.
Excerpt from *Wed at Leisure* copyright © 2014 by Sabrina Darby.

EPub Edition JUNE 2014 ISBN: 9780062336781

Print Edition ISBN: 9780062336798

AM 10 9 8 7 6 5 4 3 2 1

Chapter One

THE SINGLE-TAIL WHIP sliced through the air, leaving behind the thirteenth bloody line on a canvas of black and blue skin.

Did she understand the significance?

"Please," she begged, her blond hair muffling the sweet music of her cries. Her body shook as she whimpered and moaned in agony.

No, she had no idea.

She would.

Soon.

With the hunting knife in hand, he stalked to her and pressed it against her carotid. He inhaled the pungent scent of fear emanating from her sweat-soaked pores. "Do you like my new knife? I bought it for you."

She shuddered. Oh yes, she definitely enjoyed his newest acquisition. Too bad he wouldn't be able to keep it.

Prone and hog-tied with thick blue rope that criss-crossed over her face and knotted around her arched neck, she waited for his next move, blood trickling from the soles of her feet as a result of the final lash. She panted, her lungs barely inflating.

After a brutal beating with both a cane and whip, most in her position would have tired and dropped their neck, strangling themselves on the rope. Her strength and determination surprised him.

Perhaps she required another challenge.

He rested his knife on the bed beside her and picked up his black duffel bag. Rummaging through it, he found the final torture and smiled. The thick, four-inch-tall, white leather posture collar would look beautiful on her. He buckled it around her neck, squeezing her windpipe with the rope.

"Why?" she gasped, the porcelain skin of her face reddening from the lack of oxygen to her blood.

"What motivates anyone to kill?" He lifted the knife. "There's greed." He carved several shallow cuts on her torso. "Envy, anger, passion, self-defense, necessity."

She stared at him in horror.

That simply wouldn't do.

"Identification." With a lover's touch, he gently shut her eyelids. "But we can't forget the two most important reasons," he whispered, slashing the bare mound between her legs.

"Revenge."

She remained silent, her body frozen and her skin a mottled bluish hue. His eyes teared at the realization that he'd never feel her lips on him again.

"And mercy."

Then he plunged his new hunting knife straight into her nonbeating heart.

Chapter Two

Fourteen Days to Elections...

AFTER THREE HOURS of computer research on piercing the corporate veil, Kate's vision blurred, the words on the screen bleeding into one another until they resembled a giant Rorschach inkblot. She lowered her mug of lukewarm coffee to her cubicle's mahogany tabletop and rubbed her tired eyes.

Without warning, the door to the interns' windowless office flew open, banging against the wall. Light streamed into the dim room, casting the elongated shadow of her boss, Nicholas Trenton, on the beige carpet.

"Ms. Martin, take your jacket and come with me." He didn't wait for a response, simply issued his command and strode down the hall.

Jumping to her feet, she teetered on her secondhand heels and grabbed her suit jacket from the back of her chair. As Mr. Trenton's intern for the year, she'd follow him off the edge of a cliff. She had no choice in the matter if she wanted a junior associate position at Detroit's most prestigious law firm, Joseph and Long, after graduation. Because of the fierce competition for an internship and because several qualified lackeys waited patiently in the wings for an opening, one minor screwup would result in termination.

Most of the other interns ignored the interruption, but her best friend Hannah took a second to raise an arched eyebrow. Kate shrugged, having no idea what her boss required. He hadn't spoken to her since her initial interview a few months earlier.

She collected her briefcase, her heart pounding. As far as she knew, she hadn't made a mistake since starting two months ago. Other than class time, she'd spent virtually every waking moment at this firm, a schedule her boyfriend, Tom, resented. To placate him, she'd used her dinner break last Saturday to drive to his place and give him a quick blow job before returning to work. She didn't even have time for her own orgasm.

She raced as fast as she could down the hallway and found her boss pacing and talking on his cell phone in the marbled lobby. He frowned and pointedly looked at his watch, demonstrating his displeasure at her delay. Still on the phone, he stalked out of the firm and headed toward the elevator. She chased him, cursing her short legs as she remained a step or two behind until catching up with him in the elevator.

When the doors slid shut, he ended his call and slipped his cell into the pocket of his Armani jacket. She risked a quick glance at him to ascertain his mood, careful not to visually suggest anything more than casual regard.

He was an extremely handsome man whose picture frequently appeared in local magazines and papers beside prominent judges and legislative officials. But photos couldn't do him justice, film lacking the capability of capturing his commanding presence. Often she'd had to fight her instinct to look directly into his blue eyes. At the office, his every move, his every word overshadowed anyone and everything around her.

Standing close to him in the claustrophobic space, she inhaled the musky scent of his aftershave, felt his radiating heat. Her trembling body instinctively angled toward him.

Mr. Trenton spoke, fracturing the quiet of the small space with his deep and powerful voice. "This morning, our firm's biggest client, Jaxon Deveroux, arrived home from his business trip and found his wife dead from multiple stab wounds."

"I thought you limited your practice to civil law," she blurted out before she could stop herself. When his jaw grew rigid, she internally chastised herself for the mistake. "Sorry, sir. I shouldn't have interrupted."

The silence was deafening as she waited for him to decide whether to accept her apology. Interns had been fired for less.

"No, you shouldn't have interrupted. However, it was a valid question and, therefore, I'll let it pass."

Once the elevator doors opened, they stepped out into the bustling main floor lobby, and she fought to match

Mr. Trenton's brisk pace as they headed toward the parking garage. "While typically I would refer my clients to Jeffrey Reaver, the head of our criminal division, Mr. Deveroux and I have been friends for many years, and he requested me personally. Jaxon's a very private man, but those who are in his circle are aware of certain…proclivities that may come up in the police's line of questioning."

What sort of proclivities? It pained her to remain silent.

He paused as if expecting her to screw up by asking another question. She curled the sharp edges of her nails into the flesh of her palms, the biting pain a reminder to keep her mouth shut. A wave of peace rippled through her, and her heart slowed for the first time since Mr. Trenton had requested her presence.

"He and his wife engaged in the practice of BDSM. Do you know what that is, Ms. Martin?" he asked with a slight upturn of his lips. On anyone else, she'd believe it was the beginning of a smile, but since she'd never seen Mr. Trenton smile, she couldn't be sure what it meant.

There wasn't a woman in the country who hadn't heard of BDSM since the popular erotica novel hit the charts a few years back. His mention of it awoke that dormant part of her hibernating in the recesses of her mind during the light of day.

Her cheeks heated, but she kept her tone professional despite the fireworks launching between her thighs. "BDSM stands for bondage and discipline, domination and submission, sadism and masochism. It's kinky sex."

They reached the parking garage and climbed the concrete stairs to the second level.

"For some it is, and for others, it's a way of life. Unfortunately, the media has a way of distorting the truth to their advantage for the sensational headlines. You remember the recent case."

A metro-Detroit man had allegedly hired a hit man to kill his wife, but it was the fact that he'd practiced BDSM in a seedy sex dungeon that the media had latched on to, riding the frenzy caused by the popular erotica trilogy.

Kate had read the books. Twice. But in the end, she agreed with the popular opinion that BDSM fiction was nothing but romantic fantasy.

A bit breathless from her attempt to keep up with him, she was relieved to slide into the passenger seat of his Mercedes. Moments later they sped toward the highway.

Weighing the consequences against her curiosity, she decided to risk asking her boss a question. "In your opinion, should Mr. Deveroux divulge the nature of his relationship with his wife to the police?"

He tilted his head as if to think over the answer, but she didn't doubt he'd known the answer before she'd finished asking the question. "At this point, I see no reason why he needs to say anything about it. What happens behind closed doors is none of their business unless it's relevant to the murder. Until someone brings it up in questioning, I'd advise Jaxon to keep his sex life to himself."

For the next few minutes, they rode in silence, and she peered out the window at Detroit's crumbling houses. The car proceeded west to the suburbs and the view changed to a large brick wall that shielded homeowners and businesses from the sight of the expressway. They exited onto a street that led them into a recently developed upper-class neighborhood of palatial homes, strip malls, and trendy restaurants.

Mr. Trenton turned the car into the parking lot of a police station, which was inconspicuously nestled between two office buildings made of the same dark-brown brick. Had it not been for the crammed lot filled with police cars and media vans, she would've never guessed they'd reached their destination.

Of course the media had jumped on this. A white woman from the suburbs was murdered. That kind of juicy story trumped the mundane coverage of the upcoming November elections.

As her boss searched for a place to park, she watched four local news crews rushing around, several of them on cell phones, no doubt calling their contacts for more information on the murder.

Vultures.

Mr. Trenton gripped the door handle. "Did you take advanced criminal procedure in school, Ms. Martin?"

"No, sir. Why?"

"Some of the details you'll both hear and witness today may be graphic. Since the class prepares students by desensitizing them with real crime photos of stab wounds and gunshots, I thought you might be more prepared for what you're about to encounter."

She bit the inside of her cheek, tamping down the vivid image of blood-splattered leaves and the sulfuric scent of gunpowder. "It won't bother me."

There was no mistaking that her answer had caused him to grin. "I didn't think it would. I wouldn't have allowed you to accompany me if I hadn't thought you were up for it, but I needed to confirm. It wouldn't look good if my intern fainted over a couple of crime scene photos."

They departed the Mercedes, and this time Mr. Trenton walked beside her, escorting her inside the police station to the information desk, where he handed a young male officer a business card from his pocket. "Please let Mr. Deveroux know his attorney is here."

The cop picked up a desk phone and pressed an extension. "Is Mr. Deveroux expecting a Nicholas Trenton?"

She hadn't stepped into a police station in ten years, but the memory of that harrowing day crashed into her with the force and velocity of a gunshot. Her chest tightened as she tried to breathe. In an attempt to ward off the anxiety attack, she counted backward from one hundred.

Her boss leaned over and whispered in her ear. "You're okay. Breathe through your nose."

Pressing her lips together, she sucked air through her nose, expanding her lungs with precious oxygen. *How had he known?*

"Thank you," the officer said into the phone. He hung up, picked up a notebook, flipped it open, and handed Mr. Trenton a pen. "You two need to sign in."

Her boss signed his name before giving her the pen. Hands shaking, she supplied her barely legible information. After she gave back the notebook, the officer buzzed them in and pointed behind him. "Go through those doors to room three, second room on the left."

As Mr. Trenton stepped in front of her, she surreptitiously obtained a small pill from her Tic Tac dispenser in her purse and slipped it in her mouth. When they got to the interrogation room, he knocked on the door.

Anticipation boiled in her blood. Something was wrong with how eager she was to meet her client, a man who would find himself under suspicion of his wife's murder even if he was innocent of the crime.

Could she defend a man if she believed he was guilty?

As the door opened and her sight fell on the man hunched over a table, she had a feeling she'd soon find out.

Chapter Three

IF JAXON DEVEROUX had killed his wife, he was one hell of an actor.

He lifted his head, the despair and strain from the tragedy evident in his bloodshot brown eyes and pallid face. His thick, wavy black hair was in desperate need of a cut, and, judging by the dark stubble on his chin and cheeks, he'd obviously skipped shaving this morning. A faded, jagged scar through his left brow added to his allure.

He was still the most beautiful man she'd ever seen.

She hadn't made the connection from his name, but she recognized him as one of the men standing next to Mr. Trenton in a picture she had clipped from a magazine. A local children's hospital had dedicated a wing in the Deveroux name after his venture capital firm had donated $20 million. The confident glint in his eyes had captivated her even through the photograph.

He eyed her warily before his tortured gaze rested on his friend, communicating a silent plea for help. "Nick. Lyssa's dead. Someone—"

"Jaxon, don't say another word." Her boss marched ahead of her into the room as if he'd done it a thousand times before. "Nicholas Trenton, attorney for Jaxon Deveroux."

A gray-haired, potbellied detective stood to greet him. "Detective Lawrence."

He shook her boss's hand and then gripped the door handle, preparing to close it. She edged her way into the room seconds before it shut with a reverberating click.

Resting along the wall, she carefully appraised the space. It appeared almost identical to the one she'd set foot in ten years ago. No bigger than twelve by ten, the room contained three folding chairs and a rectangular metal table bolted to the worn beige linoleum floor.

Mr. Trenton tossed her a perfunctory glance as he sat beside Mr. Deveroux. "This is my assistant, Kate Martin." He directed his attention to the detective who had positioned himself at the head of the table. "I assume you took Mr. Deveroux's statement at the scene?"

Not having a chair in which to sit, she didn't know what to do with herself. She couldn't interrupt or Mr. Trenton would likely fire her, but he had brought her to work. With no alternative, she crouched and quietly unzipped her briefcase, retrieving a pen and legal pad to begin taking notes.

The detective nodded. "We did. He didn't ask for a law—"

"I'll want a copy of that statement."

She watched her boss closely, marveling at the way he spoke with confident authority despite his inexperience in criminal law.

"Of course," responded the cop, his lips curled with derision. "We'll get it to you as soon as possible."

Her heart continued to beat wildly from the combination of the resurgence of long-forgotten memories, the danger of standing in a testosterone-laden room with loaded guns, and a man suspected of brutally stabbing his wife to death.

Her boss softened his demeanor and lowered his voice. "What is the status of Mrs. Deveroux?"

"We're currently still processing the body. The M.E. will transfer it within a couple of hours after my men have completed taking their photos."

Mr. Deveroux slapped his hand on the table, startling her with his sudden outburst. "That body is my wife, Detective. She is not an *it*," he shouted and then muttered under his breath almost to himself, "She never was."

The room grew uncomfortably silent except for the laughter coming from the hallway and the quiet buzzing of the florescent lights. Torn between the inappropriate urge to applaud him for having the guts to speak up for his wife against the insensitive officer and the even more inappropriate desire to wrap her arms around him to console him, she did neither and instead chewed on the cap of her pen.

Detective Lawrence tipped his head to the side and folded his hands in front of him on the table in an obvious attempt at appearing remorseful. "Jaxon, I'm very sorry about the loss of your wife. I assure you, I will find the person responsible. I realize you've already answered some questions at your home, but I'm going to have to ask them again for the record. But in order to do my job to the best of my ability, I need you to be honest with me. If you don't understand a question, please let me know and I'll rephrase it for you. This interview is being video recorded as is our precinct's policy. Do you understand?"

Mr. Deveroux shifted in his chair and crossed his legs. "Yes. But before we begin, will you please get Ms. Martin a chair? I do believe the young woman is part of my legal team and, therefore, has earned the right to sit at my side during this interview."

Squirming, she tried to flatten herself against the wall. Both the detective and her boss glared at her as if they'd forgotten she was in the room. Maybe they had. But not Jaxon. Her chest filled with a foreign sensation, something bubbly, like she'd drunk a pop too fast.

As Detective Lawrence left the room, she pretended to examine the dusty floor, unable to find the courage to check if Mr. Trenton's expression registered his disappointment.

This internship meant the world to her, and she'd do anything to keep it. She'd tracked Nicholas Trenton's career since he'd made headlines by becoming a full senior partner in the state's top law firm at age thirty, a feat never accomplished by anyone before or since. At that time, she'd been a junior in college with aspirations of becoming an attorney, and she'd chosen him as her future mentor. Everything she'd done in undergraduate and law school was in preparation to work by his side.

Detective Lawrence returned and placed the additional folding chair next to Mr. Trenton. He sat, annoyance evident in every wrinkle on his face. "I need you to tell me everything that happened in the last twenty-four hours leading up to the time you found your wife."

She forced herself to keep her head held high as she took her seat, telling herself she belonged here. With Jaxon's acknowledgment of her, she almost believed it.

Jaxon slid a questioning glance at Mr. Trenton, who nodded his permission to speak.

"Up until this morning…" His voice caught, and he coughed, clearing his throat. "I was in Chicago on business. Yesterday I had a breakfast meeting in the morning with potential investors and spent the afternoon closing a deal at the firm of Lebowitz, Hoffmyer, and Gold. I ate dinner in my hotel room around seven. This morning, I woke early and drove home." He paused. "I came in through the garage, and Lyssa's car was still there. I was surprised because she has a standing appointment to have her nails done every Tuesday morning, but I wasn't worried." He slid his wedding ring up and down his finger. "I called out her name as I climbed the stairs, and she didn't respond. When I entered the bedroom…I… she was…" Her boss placed a hand on Jaxon's back and whispered something in his ear.

After a long moment of silence, Detective Lawrence sat back in his chair. "I know this is hard for you. Take your time. Would you like a glass of water?"

"No." Jaxon coughed again. "I…want to finish." He took a breath, shuddered, and stared at the blank white wall in front of him, although Kate got the feeling he was seeing something else. Or rather…someone. "Her hands and feet were bound with blue rope. She was on her stomach, a white collar around her neck. Covered in blood. I ran to her to check if she was still breathing. The collar…kept me from accessing her pulse point. I touched her wrists; they were purple…but the ropes covered the pulse, so I tried to untie her." He paused. "I couldn't. She didn't move. Didn't breathe. I knew I was too late. I took my cell phone from my pocket and called nine-one-one. Then I left her there and went downstairs to wait for the police. That's it."

Kate recognized the anguish in his dark eyes, having seen the same look in hers every time she stared in the mirror. He didn't cry, but every word from his lips was laced with sorrow and regret. She hadn't cried either all those years ago. Her old therapist had said once she got over the shock, all the emotions she'd suppressed would eventually boil over and pour out of her.

She was still waiting.

"Thank you, Jaxon. I know that was hard and I appreciate you telling your story," Detective Lawrence said in a soft tone. "Now I need to clarify a few things. When did you leave for Chicago?"

"We need you to clarify a few things for us, Katie." The burly detective grinned at her, his yellow teeth reminding her of Uncle Tate's. Both men smelled of chewing tobacco.

"I want to see my mom." She needed to explain that it wasn't her fault before the police told their version.

The detective peered over his shoulder at the pretty female cop standing in front of the door, keeping her hostage. The cop shook her head, and he glanced back at Katie. "She's on her way, but we can't allow you to see her until you tell us the truth."

Why wouldn't they believe her? She clenched her blood-soaked hands. *"I told you the truth. I want to go home."*

"Sunday morning." Jaxon's deep voice brought Kate back to the present. She subtly brushed her chin against her shoulder to check if her boss had noticed her momentary lapse of attention.

"Where did you stay?" Detective Lawrence asked.

Jaxon rubbed his forehead. "The Waldorf Astoria on Walton."

Kate's knee bounced under the table. She clutched her hands on her thighs and pinched the flesh. Although slight, the pain worked to cease the motion.

"Did anyone stay with you?"

A muscle in Jaxon's jaw jumped. "No."

Frowning, the detective drummed his thick fingers on the table. "When did you last speak with your wife?"

Pain flashed in Jaxon's eyes, and he swallowed hard. "Before I went to sleep."

"What time was that?"

Jaxon thought it over. "Around eight or nine."

"Can anyone confirm you were in your room?"

Waiting for Jaxon's answer, Kate's pulse increased. He required a strong alibi to avoid being a suspect in the murder.

"I'm sure room service can verify I had dinner."

"And you stayed in your room all night?"

His index finger twitched. "I...went out to get ice."

"What time?"

"After I spoke with my wife."

"She had a lot of bruising on her body. Any idea of how she got that?"

"I...all I saw was the blood. She was covered in it."

"Here's a picture to remind you." Detective Lawrence slapped down an eight-by-eleven photo.

Horrified and slightly nauseous yet unable to glance away, Kate stared at the picture of Alyssa Deveroux covered in thick welts, cuts, bruises, and stab wounds.

Mr. Trenton shot to his feet. "Jaxon, we're leaving." He picked up his briefcase and slammed it on the table, yanking her fascinated attention from the photo. "You've crossed a line, Detective. He just lost his wife, and he's still in shock. To show him the crime scene photo is cruel."

The detective sat still as a rock, quiet determination simmering below the surface. "I'll do whatever it takes to find this killer even if it means upsetting your client. He's having trouble remembering some of the details. Details that may help solve this case."

"Nick, it's all right," Jaxon said, his skin so pale she could make out the blue veins underneath. "I'm fine."

But he wasn't fine. How could he be when instead of mourning, he had to defend himself to a stranger who cared nothing for Alyssa?

A heavy knock sounded. "Damn it," cursed Detective Lawrence, striding to the door and opening it to reveal a younger officer. They spoke in hushed whispers. She couldn't discern the words, but the detective stiffened.

The officer left and Detective Lawrence slunk back to his seat. He glowered at Jaxon. "The hotel confirmed you checked out using their television service at eight and left the key at the counter. Since the medical examiner has estimated time of death between four and six this morning, your alibi clears you of a murder charge, unless we learn something different. You're free to go at this time, but we may have additional questions for you in the future, and while travel is not restricted, we'd appreciate it if you could remain available while we follow the leads in your wife's death."

Jaxon exhaled. "Of course."

"Do you have anything you'd like to add before we complete this interview? Anything that may aid us in the investigation?"

He leaned across the table. "Find the monster that did this to my wife."

And in that moment, as her pill finally kicked in and eased her racing heart, she wondered when she'd started thinking of her client not as Mr. Deveroux but as Jaxon.

Chapter Four

FLASHES OF LIGHT blinded her as they stepped outside of the station. Shielding her eyes with her hand, she glimpsed the swarm of reporters, photographers, and videographers shining bright spotlights on them.

"Jaxon! Is it true you're a sadist?"

"Did you kill your wife?"

Tons of questions flew at Jaxon from every direction, the buzzards circling them as if they were rotting carcasses.

The door behind her swung open and Detective Lawrence swaggered out, his arms waving at the reporters in a half-assed attempt to get them to leave. The cop was reveling in his fifteen minutes of fame, bellowing to the frenzied crowd of blood-thirsty piranhas to "give them some space."

Anyone who defended the press as only doing their job had obviously never been subjected to the media's unapologetic barrage of emotionally charged questions or intense scrutiny. They didn't see you as human. You were a caged animal for them to poke with their sharp spears, and then they laughed when they brought you to tears.

"What happened in the woods?"

"Is it true your mother asked the assistant district attorney to try you as an adult?"

"Were you being abused?"

Like a deer staring down the barrel of a shotgun, she froze in her tracks. Dark spots floated in her eyes, and the cacophony morphed into a whooshing in her ears.

Her chest burned.

She couldn't breathe.

The clawing need to escape strangled her as the ground tilted below her numb feet and her trembling legs buckled.

And then...heat. The comforting, woodsy scent of Christmas morning surrounded her, eased her.

Reality returned and with it the persistent shouts of the reporters.

She was in front of the police station, burrowed into the woolen side of a man who felt like...home. His arm banded around her waist, supporting her. Sheltering her. This man had learned her weakness and could use it against her. But who was he?

Raising her head, she discovered the identity of her chivalrous rescuer.

Jaxon.

He peered down at her, his concern for her evident in his scotch-colored eyes. "You're safe. I won't let anyone hurt you."

She allowed herself another ten seconds of bliss before she pulled back. "I'm fine." After fidgeting with the hem of her skirt, she unzipped her purse and retrieved another pill. She slipped it on her tongue, the action itself providing some relief. Jaxon's hand cupped her shoulder. He'd already witnessed her panic attack. What difference did it make if he knew she took antianxiety medication now and then?

Bravely positioned in the middle of the crowd, Mr. Trenton projected his voice over the noisy reporters. "I'll give a brief statement, but I will not answer any questions at this time." When he captured their attention, he continued. "This morning, Jaxon Deveroux came home and found his wife's body. He called the police, has cooperated fully, and will continue to work with them to bring Alyssa Deveroux's murderer to justice. Having no bearing on this matter, the private sexual relationship between Jaxon and Alyssa Deveroux should remain exactly that: private. The focus of this investigation should be on finding the murderer and not rendering moral judgments on the Deveroux' alleged sexual practices. At this time, we ask the media to respect his wishes and allow him the opportunity to mourn his wife."

With a jab of his chin in the direction of the parking lot, Mr. Trenton signaled to them to make their move. Jaxon entwined their fingers and squeezed, silently reiterating his promise to protect her. She swallowed her fear, and he led her through the mayhem to the curb.

A man wearing a suit but resembling a linebacker held open the back door of a dark, nondescript BMW and ushered Jaxon inside. Before she could process the scene, the man jogged to the front, got into the driver's seat, and sped away.

"Private security," Mr. Trenton explained, obviously noticing Kate's confusion, and he hustled her, his hand on her elbow, to his car. The reporters scattered to their vehicles in an effort to follow Jaxon.

One of the perks of being an overnight celebrity. Loss of privacy.

The media didn't care if you hadn't asked to be a celebrity. Didn't care if you just lost the only person who ever loved you. Didn't care if you were fourteen. They thrust you in the limelight. They may have blacked out your face and left out your name, but everyone knew it was you. You couldn't hide. So you stopped hiding and gave them a show.

When they arrived back at the firm's parking structure, he placed the car in park and shifted his weight in his seat to face her.

She bit the inside of her cheek as he studied her intently. She waited for the inevitable.

"I'm going pass some of your existing caseload to Hannah."

And there it was. "I'm sorry for drawing attention in the interrogation room. If you give me another chance, I promise to do better."

Small creases formed on his forehead. "Why are you apologizing?"

"You just fired me."

The creases smoothed, replaced by wrinkles around his eyes. "You misunderstood, Ms. Martin. I want you to second chair on the Deveroux matter. I can already anticipate Jaxon's case taking up much of your time. It's got to be your top priority at work."

Relieved, she let out the breath she hadn't realized she'd been holding. He hadn't fired her. In fact, she'd have the chance to work even closer with him and learn the potential complexities of a criminal case. "Why wouldn't you have Mr. Reaver second chair? After all, he has the experience—"

He frowned. "Jaxon doesn't want Reaver. He wants me and I want you. I shouldn't tell you this, but when you submitted your resume to become my intern, Reaver fought to have you assigned to him. After all, it's not every day we get a National Criminal Law Trial Advocacy champion applying for an internship at Joseph and Long."

Not since Nick. According to the interviews she'd read, the competition had given him the edge he'd needed to win a coveted slot as Miles Joseph's intern. Which was why she also entered the competition. "I would have turned him down since I have no interest in pursuing a career in criminal law."

He nodded. "That's what I told him. You obviously have a gift in the courtroom whether you ultimately choose civil or criminal law. I'm offering you a chance to put your gift to work. Not for a trophy and a couple hundred dollars but for real. This will make your career. You'll have every law firm in the country clamoring to hire you when you graduate next summer. I believe in you. You're fully capable of handling this case. I wouldn't risk my best friend's freedom."

Second chair meant she'd be the second in command, a position typically reserved for a senior attorney or more advanced associates. As Mr. Trenton's right hand, she'd be responsible for research and motion preparation, depositions, exhibits, and trial prep. And if Jaxon went to trial, she'd sit beside Mr. Trenton in the courtroom. Although she was an intern, she'd be permitted to examine the witnesses. Excitement shot through her. "I know you wouldn't, and I appreciate you having faith in me."

"There's something about you that goes beyond the mere intelligence and drive I've seen in previous interns. You remind me of myself at your age."

He didn't know he'd just paid her the highest compliment. How embarrassed would she be if he discovered she idolized him to the point of collecting clippings of him throughout the years? "Thank you."

"Ms. Martin, may I call you Kate?"

His voice went slightly husky and her body responded, her nipples tightening beneath her lacy bra. "Yes, sir."

"When we're alone, you can call me Nick." Her heart danced when he reached his hand out as if he was going to touch her. At the last second, he relaxed it on the headrest inches from her shoulder. "I've watched you this month. You don't take care of yourself. You don't take breaks for meals, and when you do, they're in the form of vending machine foods and coffee."

She shivered. "How do you know that?"

"I told you. I've watched you." His gaze dropped to her mouth and then up to her eyes once more.

Was she imagining the sparks between them? What was wrong with her to have such a strong attraction to both her boss and her client? Both men were completely off-limits. Besides, she was in love with Tom. Wasn't she?

"There's another reason you remind me of myself at your age. I was also eager to prove myself. You're at your desk when I leave at night and you're there when I arrive in the morning." He said it as if it were a bad thing.

"And look where that hard work got you."

"What it got me was a bleeding ulcer and a few days in the hospital. The thing about control is that it's limited. We don't choose to get sick and we certainly can't choose not to vomit blood during finals."

Her jaw dropped. "Did that really happen?"

"Yes. It was the fall semester of my third year, and I was in the same spot as you: an intern at Joseph and Long, only I worked for Miles Joseph. If you think I'm a taskmaster, you should try interning for him for a week. I lived off coffee and donuts. I didn't get more than four or five hours of sleep a night, and I popped Tums like they were candy. Who had time to stop and worry about stomach pain and a little blood when my career was at stake? I was in the middle of my ethics exam when it happened. I didn't even make it to the bathroom. Vomited blood all over the guy next to me and then passed out cold. Woke up in the hospital and all I cared about was I hadn't finished my exam. They had to sedate me to keep me from leaving."

Although she'd like to think she was different, she would've done the same. "Wouldn't your professor allow you to take the exam?"

"Of course. Attorneys aren't complete sadists," he said with a straight face. Then he laughed. "Sorry, bad joke." He continued, shrugging. "I wasn't rational. Then Mr. Joseph paid me a visit in the hospital. I thought he'd fire me. Instead, he sat down in the chair next to my bed and told me a story about how he'd gotten so successful. All the typical bullshit about studying hard, kissing ass, and exploring as many opportunities as life presented. He wished me well and then got up and started walking out, but he stopped at the door. He turned around, raised one finger, and said, 'In the end, you always have to watch out for yourself.'"

"That was nice of him."

"Yes," he said, nodding. "*Then* he fired me."

He said it so casually, she didn't believe him. "No, you're lying."

"I'm not lying."

There had to be a moral to this story. "He fired you because you were working too hard, right?"

"No." He dropped his hand from the headrest onto her shoulder and squeezed it. "He fired me because I couldn't do my job while in the hospital, which meant I couldn't get him the brief he needed, resulting in him having to explain to the judge why it wasn't submitted on time. Let's face it: the judges don't give a shit what your excuse is. He got extra time, but I'd made him look bad. He had to fire me because he had to look out for himself first."

Her shoulder tingled from the brief contact of his warm hand. "That's cruel. You couldn't help it. You were in the hospital."

"If I had taken better care of myself, gotten more sleep, eaten healthy, listened to what my body was trying to tell me, I wouldn't have ended up with a bleeding ulcer, and I wouldn't have disappointed Mr. Joseph. He did me a favor when he fired me because I never made that kind of mistake again. I learned to take care of my own needs first."

"It worked out for you. You ended up as senior partner, so Mr. Joseph and you must have stayed friendly."

He huffed. "I don't think anyone could call Mr. Joseph friendly. But we each had something to gain by working with the other, and so we've maintained an *amicable* relationship throughout the years." Nick's emphasis on the word amicable made her think it wasn't amicable at all. "I don't want you ending up like me. Learn from my mistakes. I don't expect you to work more than ten hours a day, including meals, Monday through Friday, unless I specifically request it. And by meals, I don't mean coffee and a bag of pretzels. After work, go home, relax, and get a good night's sleep. Your weekends are yours, but don't overdo the fun. You don't want to drag yourself in on Monday too sluggish to give me your all."

How long had it been since she'd gone to a movie with Tom or to the bar with friends? She couldn't remember a weekend she hadn't spent in the office.

"I don't think I'm on my way to an ulcer, but I appreciate the advice. When I applied for the internship, I never expected to have the opportunity to learn so much. I thought I'd spend the year as your lemming." She tried to pass it off as a joke, but she wasn't kidding. Since her first term in law school, she'd learned everything she could about Nicholas Trenton. The phrase she heard over and over was "sadistic taskmaster." In exchange for gaining the experience as his intern, you gave up life as you knew it. He owned you. Now she wondered if it was all a way to limit the competition for the position. Because if anything, Nick was proving to be the opposite.

"As your mentor and your boss, it's my responsibility to ensure you learn balance. This career can swallow you whole if you allow it. I don't want that to happen to you." Something resembling interest flickered in his eyes, but it quickly disappeared, leaving her to wonder if she'd imagined it. "Go home, get some rest, and if something comes up with the case, I'll give you a call. Keep your cell phone near you even at night. I'll see you at nine tomorrow morning."

She gathered her things, and as she slammed the car door shut, she thought she heard him say, "Sweet dreams, Kate."

His last words still ringing in her ears, she carried her briefcase toward the cars and, knowing he was watching, took out her keys as she stood in front of a black Ford Fusion. She waved to him, giving the all clear for him to leave.

When he drove away and she could no longer see him, she strolled to her bike that was tucked into the corner of the garage. She slid into the leather pants she kept in the saddlebag and shimmied off her skirt. After changing into boots, she dropped her work attire into the saddlebag, placed her briefcase in the luggage rack, and swung her leg over the seat.

This was her baby.

Her teal-and-black 2000 Harley Davidson Sportster. Not the most badass ride, but for a sixteen-year-old who'd just gotten her license and had no other way of getting where she needed to go, it had been a necessity.

And she owed it all to her best friend from home, Caden. When she'd gone off the rails in high school, he'd been the only person who remained her friend, and since he was gay, he'd also been one of the only guys in her small school she hadn't messed around with. Caden hadn't judged her during that phase. Just made sure she had an ample supply of condoms.

Trying to keep her out of trouble, he taught her everything she needed to know about motorcycles, and together they fixed up the Sportster and rebuilt the engine. But afterward she'd kept up on the maintenance of the bike herself and had driven it twelve hours from the Upper Peninsula down to metro Detroit when she moved here for college. Sucked on rainy and snowy days, but if she needed a ride, she'd get one from Hannah or take the People Mover, Detroit's version of Chicago's L.

She never felt freer than when she was on the back of her baby. And tonight, she needed to feel free more than ever. Although she appreciated Nick's advice on taking care of herself, she hadn't gone out with her friends since the summer. He'd ordered her to go home, but a girl had to eat, right? Besides, she had nothing in her fridge.

Decision made, she slipped her cell from her pocket and dialed.

Hannah answered on the first ring. "What the hell happened to you?"

"I don't want to talk over the phone." She smiled. "Want to meet for a drink?"

Chapter Five

KATE WINCED AS she squeezed in between two burly men dressed in Detroit Lions jerseys standing by the entrance of the bar. "Excuse me," she shouted over the bar's piped-in music.

The bar was packed tonight. She hadn't stepped foot inside since she'd started her internship. Staring at a sea of singles, she realized she hadn't missed this place. Still, she'd enjoy spending time with her friends.

The downtown bar was centrally located, making it easily accessible to three universities as well as two arenas. Decorated with Detroit sports memorabilia, it prided itself on being the number-one sports bar in the state. She'd call it a meat market with overpriced, spoiled meat. But the food was good and the bartenders could fix her drink right, which gained the bar several points in her book. Too many times she'd garnered a blank stare when asking for a Sloe Gin Fizz. These days, girls drank

Sex on the Beach and Flaming Orgasms. Standard drinks were considered relics.

Guess she was an old-fashioned girl at heart.

She scanned the room, but at five-foot-three, she couldn't see over the people standing around the bar. Chances were good Hannah had nabbed a small table in the back.

Spotting Hannah sitting with a couple of other interns from the firm, she thought about inviting Tom. He'd probably be getting off his shift now at the hospital, and, with her new schedule, they hadn't spent much time together lately. She couldn't wait to tell him about Nick requesting she work with him on the Deveroux case.

Hannah waved at Kate. "Hey, sis. We were just talking about you. I can't believe you're actually here. I thought you'd officially moved into the law firm."

Back in the first year of school, Hannah had begun calling her "sis" when a couple of guys had mistaken them for twins because they both had long, wavy blond hair, blue eyes, and petite builds. But although she adored her friend, Kate had never felt comfortable returning the sentiment. Maybe because she didn't have the best history with her family.

As soon as she dropped into her chair, the waitress came by and Kate ordered two Sloe Gin Fizzes, figuring she'd save the girl an extra trip. When the waitress left, Kate said, "I had to go out for sustenance at some point. You can take only so much of watered-down coffee and cookies before you start craving a vegetable or two."

"Well, if it's vegetables you're craving, David here is an excellent couch potato, and when he's drunk a couple of beers, Logan gets rather corny."

She recognized David Washington and Logan Bradford as interns from Joseph and Long. They didn't work with Hannah and Kate in the "bat cave," the name coined by previous interns for the room due to its lack of windows. David and Logan interned for criminal defense attorneys and worked in the "cafeteria," a room with plenty of natural sunlight, its own coffeemaker, a refrigerator, and a microwave. Kate had passed by it on her way to the copy room and was surprised by the sounds of laughter coming from inside. Almost made her wish she'd chosen to pursue criminal law.

David hooked an arm over Hannah's shoulder and squeezed her. "Funny, Hannah Banana. What kind of law are you planning on practicing? Entertainment law? Because you always entertain me."

David was older than Kate by a few years, heavy-set yet handsome with a dimple in his chin, laughing blue eyes, and black curly hair. He reminded her of a teddy bear, but she'd heard through the grapevine that he had one hell of a growl. Logan, on the other hand, was tall and lean, with a buzz cut and serious brown eyes. Closer to Nick's age, he'd spent a few years in the army before attending law school and still looked every bit the military man. She was glad to finally meet some of the other interns out of the office.

"Family law," answered Hannah. "Although if Ryan Gosling sought my expertise, I wouldn't turn him down."

"I bet you wouldn't," Kate said wryly.

The waitress returned with the drinks, and Kate started in on hers immediately, relishing the burn of the alcohol down her throat.

"Speaking of celebrities, we caught the six o'clock news at the firm," said Hannah. "You clean up good on camera, although they got only a couple of brief shots of you standing behind Mr. Trenton. So we're dying to know. What happened?"

David and Logan stopped chatting. She shouldn't feel awkward, but she did, as if she were in the spotlight on stage, giving her debut performance. "Obviously I can't get into the specifics of the case, but Mr. Trenton brought me to Mr. Deveroux's police interview."

David crossed his arms and sat back in his chair. "I'm surprised they haven't arrested him yet."

"Why's that?" she asked.

"Oh, come on. It's far more likely Deveroux did it over a stranger. He probably got carried away while they were getting their kink on and killed her. I mean, who else would have bound her naked in their bed?"

A feeling of unease spread through her. "How did you know she was bound naked?"

He gave her a quizzical glance. "The news. They did a whole report on S&M, and Friday night they're airing a special on the seedy side of underground sex clubs. As if there's a sunny side to them."

She pulled out her cell phone and started dialing. "I should call Nick."

"Why?" Hannah asked.

"He should know about the media."

"I'm sure he does," Logan said, plucking the cell from Kate's hand. "He didn't get to where he's gotten by being ignorant. I'm sure if he needs you, you'll get a call. After all, you're his intern."

She retrieved the phone from Logan and tossed it in her purse. "So is Hannah, but he didn't bring her to the police station." As soon as the words left her lips, she realized her error, not intending to have insulted her friend.

Hannah waved her beautifully manicured fingers in the air. "He knows I'm squeamish from my initial interview. That's why I'm going into civil law rather than criminal. He was being considerate of me."

David snorted and muttered, "If you say so."

"I'm sure he'll include you if anything else happens," Kate said to Hannah in an attempt to rectify her mistake.

David brandished a hundred-dollar bill in front of them. "I'll put a hundred bucks down that the DA will issue an arrest warrant by Halloween. You guys in?"

Hannah laughed, but Logan had the decency to frown at his friend and tell him to put his money away. Kate didn't understand how anyone could make light of murder. She reeled in her temper and took another sip of her drink. These were her co-workers after all.

"The police won't arrest Jaxon Deveroux because he's not guilty and has an alibi to prove it," she argued. "I'm sure they'll find evidence that will lead them to the perpetrator and justice will prevail. I mean, there's no such thing as a perfect crime."

Logan shook his head. "Kate, you've watched too many crime procedurals. Do you know how many homicides go unsolved in Detroit? Something like seventy-five percent. Trust me, if you want to commit a murder, do it here."

In high school, she'd obsessed over grisly homicides, but she'd never come across that statistic. "Alyssa Deveroux was killed in the suburbs."

"Still," Logan began, animatedly using his hands as he spoke, "even if the perp left behind evidence, the police have to find it and process it. Budgets are tight and people are incompetent. If they don't find the killer in the next two weeks, the chances of them solving the case go way down, and you know the media is going to scare everyone into thinking they're the next victim. They're going to go hard after your client whether he's guilty or not. Remember the JonBenet Ramsey case? Case went cold, so everyone assumed it was the mom, the dad, the brother. Ruined their fucking lives."

It was difficult enough on a local level, but at least she hadn't been in the international spotlight like the Ramseys. "You're telling me if they don't find another suspect in two weeks they're going to arrest my client?"

"David was right about one thing," said Logan. "You've got until the first week of November."

"Elections." She peered at the table and realized she'd already finished her first drink and had started on her second.

"Yeah," Logan said, nodding. "High-profile case like this, every official up for reelection within a twenty-mile radius of the crime is going to use this case to their advantage. But the real battle's gonna come from the district attorney's office. Mason Ford's campaigning on county prosecutor Savage's soft position on domestic violence and sex crimes. He fucked up a couple years back, decided not to prosecute a guy suspected of hitting his wife because the wife refused to testify. Guy got released and shot his wife dead that night before turning the gun on himself."

The pressure of public scrutiny always weighed heavy on elected legal professions such as judges and prosecutors, especially on the county level. One wrong decision could ruin a career. This meant not only did they have to do their jobs to the best of their abilities, they had to worry about their next campaign and whether their choices would result in the unseating of their position come election time.

Logan had a pleasant demeanor despite his grim warning. She immediately liked the man. "You intern for Reaver, don't you?" She finished off her second drink, feeling the subtle buzz of its effects. Hannah and David were laughing and, from Kate's point of view, looked a bit cozier than typical co-workers. Although she had hoped to spend this time catching up with her friend, she was glad to have the opportunity to talk with someone knowledgeable in criminal law.

Trying to get the waitress's attention, Logan lifted his empty beer bottle into the air. "Gotta say, I'm surprised Trenton doesn't want Reaver on this case."

"I wouldn't say Nick doesn't want him. It's the client's choice."

"You got lucky. Here I'm working for one of the top defense attorneys in the state, and you get the case of the decade," he said with a glint in his eye that told her he was teasing. "But seriously, if you need any help or have any questions, I'm your guy."

"Thanks. I may take you up on it." Although she'd prepared for a fictitious criminal trial in the National Criminal Law Trial Advocacy contest, she didn't have experience practicing the skills on a real case. It would be great if she could turn to Logan with a question now and then. So long as Nick didn't find her incompetent.

"So, it's Nick now?" Hannah asked, leaning forward from David's embrace with a smile Kate had come to know as Hannah's display of sweet before she went in for the kill. Very effective in both picking up men and crucifying a witness on the stand.

She tried to play dumb. "What are you talking about?"

"Twice you've referred to Mr. Trenton as Nick."

Normally Kate would confide in Hannah and tell her all about how Nick had treated her as an equal, complimenting her on her abilities, and how he'd almost seemed as though he was flirting with her. But she didn't want to hurt Hannah's feelings since, technically, they were competing for a spot as associate attorney at the firm next year. Not to mention she didn't want to embarrass herself by misconstruing Nick's personal intentions toward her. For now she'd keep it to herself. "He said I could call him that out of the office, and it slipped out. If it bothers you—"

"Why would it bother me? He's hot. If you and he—"

"No," she said firmly. "I'm dating Tom." *Good old reliable Tom.*

"Right. Tom." Hannah gave Kate another one of her deadly smiles. "Where is Tom tonight?"

"Probably getting off work." By now he'd have gotten home and was probably eating a bowl of Wheaties and soy milk before taking a shower to get ready for bed. She wasn't in the mood for him tonight. Kate gave Hannah her own version of a manipulative smile and pivoted her chair toward her friend. "I'll call him later, but I wanted some time with you. We haven't had a chance to hang out since we started our internships. What's new with you? Are you dating anyone?"

"Um…" Hannah blushed. Actually blushed. Kate had never seen her friend get flustered over a man.

"You are! Tell me about him."

"Well, he's really sexy," Hannah said, looking down at her lap. She waited a beat and then lifted her head, her usual confidence expressed on her flawless face. "And he's an amazing fuck."

"Hannah!"

David and Logan stopped their own conversation. Poor David blushed bright red, obviously having thought he and Hannah had something brewing and discovering he thought wrong. The men got up, David mumbling that they were going to get another drink, and they left the women alone to discuss Hannah's love life.

"What?" Hannah shrugged with a devilish grin. "He likes to experiment. His girlfriend is a dud in the sack."

"His girlfriend? You're dating someone who's got a girlfriend?"

Since meeting Hannah in first-year property class, they'd been study group partners and close friends, spending many Friday nights at the bar playing darts and drinking away the stresses of the week. Several of those evenings ended with Hannah going home with some random guy she'd met that evening. She had a frank openness about sexuality and made no apologies for it, which Kate admired. While she'd worried about Hannah's safety, her friend had never regretted going home with any of the men. But Kate was concerned that dating a taken man would end in heartbreak for Hannah.

"Big deal." Hannah's smile tightened.

Kate clutched her friend's hand. "It is a big deal. I don't want to see you get hurt."

"Please. Sex is sex. It has nothing to do with emotions. We both know where we stand, and neither one of us has made any promises. I think he gets off on pulling one over his girlfriend." Hannah removed her hand from Kate's grip and pointed her index finger. "And I get off when he does this trick with his finger in my—"

"Do not finish that sentence."

"Are you disappointed in me?"

Logan and David returned to the table with a pitcher of beer and a couple of giggling college-aged brunettes. The men scrambled to find a couple of extra chairs while Hannah and Kate continued their conversation.

"No. I mean, I don't condone it, but you're not the one in a committed relationship," Kate said, trying to believe her own argument. "He's the one cheating, and, frankly, if it wasn't with you, I'm sure it would be someone else. No offense."

"No offense taken. But to tell you the truth, he's been loyal to her in the past. He says I'm too good to pass up. Does wonders for my self-esteem."

Kate had always believed Hannah had excellent self-esteem. It was Kate who felt as if she didn't belong in the white-collar world.

"Well, then I'm glad you're happy. If something changes and you're upset, you can always count on me to be there for you. I wouldn't have gotten through law school without you by my side."

A shadow fell on the table and a deep, familiar voice from behind her said, "Didn't I tell you to go home?"

Chapter Six

KATE LOOKED OVER her shoulder at her boss, who was still dressed in the same gorgeous black Armani suit and silver tie he'd been wearing an hour ago. She had assumed he would go home for the evening. What was he doing here?

"Nick." She rose from her chair and faced her scowling boss. Shit. Kate had angered him by coming to the bar rather than going home like he'd ordered. "I thought I'd—"

He put up his hand to stop her from talking. "I don't care what you thought. I made rules for you to follow, rules that I expect you to obey if you're going to work as second chair on Jaxon's case. Apparently, you can't be trusted. Maybe Hannah would—"

"No, sir," she said a bit too forcefully. "You can count on me. I'll go home now."

Their exchange had caught the attention of the other interns as well as the girls sitting at their table. While ultimately she was an adult and didn't have to listen to her boss's orders on how to care for herself off-hours, she didn't want to disappoint him. He'd made it clear earlier he had her best intentions at heart. It didn't mean she had to like it.

Nick examined her from head to toe and back up again. "Have you had anything to drink?"

"Just a couple of Sloe Gin Fizzes. Nothing—"

"I'll drive you home and bring you back here in the morning." Before she could protest, he added, "Say goodnight to your friends."

Kate stopped moving for a moment, biting her tongue and assessing the situation from all angles. She didn't want to leave because she hadn't finished catching up with Hannah or eaten dinner yet. But was it worth it to defy him, risking her internship, her career plan, over dinner and conversation?

Her mind made up, she snagged her purse. "Goodnight," she said to Hannah, giving her and the others a little wave as she accompanied Nick out of the bar.

The room had cleared out slightly since she had arrived, but they still had to squeeze their way through the mingling singles. Approaching the front door, Nick seized her hand and pulled her through the crowd.

As soon as they got outside, she couldn't hold in her anger any longer and yanked her hand from his grip. "What is wrong with you? What makes you think you can storm into a bar like that after work hours and make demands of me in front of other interns?"

"I told you. I'm protecting you. Taking care of you since you've shown you're unable to do it for yourself. Yes, I'm your boss, but…"

He took a single step closer, making her heart pound erratically. "But?"

"I'd hoped we could be friends, Kate."

Friends. Of course. How naive to believe he had any romantic feelings toward her.

She cleared the tickle from her throat. "How did you know I was at the bar?"

"I followed you. I wanted to make sure you got home safely. Imagine my surprise when you stopped here."

His admission shocked her. It had been several years since anyone cared about her well-being enough to check up on her. Sure, she had friends such as Hannah and Caden, but even Tom didn't worry about her to the degree that he'd follow her home. Some mornings she'd left his apartment before sunrise, and he still didn't bother to call her to make sure she made it home. But she wasn't sure how she felt about Nick confronting her at the bar.

On the sidewalk, they strolled down the street and then cut behind the building to the parking lot. "I've been here for an hour and I didn't see you."

"I was watching from a nearby table."

"That's a bit…stalkerish." She laughed, but the idea that she was oblivious to him watching alarmed her. And…aroused her.

"Does it scare you?" he asked, his fingers grazing hers.

"No," she said, realizing it was true the moment it passed her lips. "But why were you watching?"

"I wanted to see you outside of the office. You're always so stiff and reserved at work. Here you were much more relaxed. You smiled. I wanted to see that."

"Oh." She supposed it was true. If they became friends, maybe she'd get to see him less formal as well. "Speaking of work, David told me the media is already running with the whole BDSM angle of the murder. They've even revealed some of the details of how she died."

He sighed. "I know. There must be a leak in the police department. We'll have to find a couple of experts to present our position that just because someone is a sadist, it doesn't mean he's a murderer."

"I don't think people will believe that. Very few people understand that in BDSM sadists inflict pain on masochists who enjoy the pain. It's easier to accept brainwashing and abuse."

When they reached the parking lot, her stomach dropped as she spotted his Mercedes next to her motorcycle.

"You seem to know a lot more about BDSM than you let on," he commented, remotely unlocking the vehicle.

"I've done some reading." A bit uncomfortable with her boss knowing anything about her secret desires, she downplayed the amount she'd researched the alternative sexual lifestyle.

"There's nothing to feel embarrassed about," he said as they got to his car. "While I'm strictly vanilla, I wouldn't judge anyone for what they enjoyed in the bedroom so long as it was consensual. Even if that person was you."

Her cheeks burned. "I'm not…I mean…I haven't. I'm vanilla too."

He chuckled. "Nothing wrong with vanilla. After all, it's the base for several other flavors." With one hand on the car's roof and the other on the handle, he said, "You know what? I'm suddenly having a craving for ice cream. Why don't we stop on the way to your apartment and I'll treat you to a scoop of vanilla?"

Ice cream sounded heavenly right now. "As long as it's a double scoop of cookie dough, you've got yourself a deal."

He raised a brow in amusement, showing a glimpse of out-of-the-office Nick. "Negotiating with me, Counselor?"

"Always."

"Do you need anything from your bike before we go?"

"Yes, I should take my briefcase," she answered slowly, anticipating a lecture. She turned around and moved to her bike, which was parked right behind her, unlocked her saddlebag, and then swung the strap of her briefcase over her shoulder.

"I can't believe you drive that thing in heels and a suit."

That wasn't the reaction she expected. "What's wrong with it?"

"Nothing. It just seems difficult to do. But you must see something wrong with it or you wouldn't have tried to hide it from me by pretending that Ford Fusion belonged to you in the firm's parking garage," he pointed out.

"Some people judge," she said, shrugging as she slid into the passenger seat of his car.

He started the ignition. "And you thought I would?"

"Yes—no—I don't know."

The car headed west toward her favorite ice cream shop. "There's nothing wrong per se with riding a motorcycle, but I can't say it doesn't concern me. Not from a professional standpoint, but as your friend. Those things are dangerous."

Once again, Nick had surprised her with his attitude. He wasn't a powerful tyrant at all. Today she'd seen several sides to him, and she liked them all.

"I've ridden for eight years, and I've never been in an accident," she said, smoothing the wrinkles of her skirt and then adding, "It's nice though."

"What is?"

Several of the day's scenes played like a home video in her mind.

Jaxon ordering the detective to bring her a chair.

Jaxon protecting her from the press.

Nick worrying about her health.

Nick troubled by her mode of transportation.

But she simply said, "Having someone care about me."

He wrenched the steering wheel, swerving the car, the tires squealing in protest. *Was there an animal in the road?* She braced her hand against the door to prevent herself from tipping, a rush of adrenaline kick-starting her pulse into overdrive.

The Mercedes came to a complete stop, propelling her weight forward and then jerking her back. Before she could ask what the hell had happened, Nick unbelted and pivoted toward her, his blue eyes like the color of the sky at twilight. "I do care." He cupped her cheek with more tenderness than she'd ever known. "Too much."

His mouth drifted closer and closer until *finally, finally, finally* his soft lips melted over hers.

She surrendered, intoxicated by his taste. On his passion.

How many years had she dreamed of this? Of him taking her under his wing and guiding her through the maze of her future, both professionally and personally?

His tongue barely grazed hers when, all too soon, he broke from their kiss, leaving her wanting, her nipples stinging, needing to be touched, and her pussy ripening, preparing for Nick's invasion.

A whisper of a moan escaped her, and she flicked the tip of her tongue over her wet bottom lip, relishing the reminder of Nick on her flesh. Then as she leaned in for more, a name sprung into her consciousness, flooding her with a tumultuous river of shame.

Tom.

Nick stroked her neck with the pad of his fingers. "Damn it, I'm sorry. I've told myself time and time again I wouldn't touch you, but the more I get to know you, the harder it is for me to resist."

She folded her trembling hands together on her lap to keep from reaching for him. "I'm seeing someone."

"Of course you are," he said, dropping his hand. "I should have known someone as beautiful as you wouldn't be available." He clicked his seatbelt and shifted the car into drive. "Please, forgive me. If you want to report me to Human Resources, I won't stop you."

"I won't," she said quickly. "There's nothing to forgive."

He pulled away from the side of the road and merged into traffic as if nothing had happened.

Meanwhile, confusion clouded her. She pressed her fingers to her swollen lips, looking for proof that she hadn't imagined the kiss. A kiss she'd wanted more than almost anything in this world.

In one day, she'd lusted over two inappropriate men and kissed one of them. What did that say about her feelings for Tom, the man she'd committed herself to more than two years ago?

And what would tomorrow bring?

Chapter Seven

Thirteen Days to Elections...

HOLDING TWO CUPS of black coffee, Kate nudged her
boss's office door open with her knee. Phone glued to his
ear, Nick stood with his back to her, facing the wall of
windows overlooking the Detroit River.

Since it had been raining when he'd picked her up
from her apartment at eight this morning, he'd bypassed
the bar and drove her straight to work, claiming he'd
return her to her bike at the end of the day. She had a feeling it was going to be a constant battle with him. Her bike
gave her the freedom to come and go on her own terms,
a luxury most people took for granted. Not her. But on a
gloomy day like this one, she didn't mind having a warm,
dry car to transport her to work.

Dressed more casual than usual in navy slacks and a
white dress shirt with the sleeves rolled up to his elbows,

he paced the length of the windows, stopping when he noticed Kate. His face was deep red, his eyes dark with rage. "Did you see the morning news?" he hissed into his cell. "Someone on your force is leaking details of the crime to the press." He pointed at the chair.

She set the coffees on the desk and bent to take her iPad from her briefcase. As she settled into her seat, she caught him watching her with an intensity that singed her. He quickly looked away, his lips pursed in response to what he'd heard from the other end of the phone.

Her insides heated like she'd downed a double shot of vodka, warmth pooling in the pit of her belly and then spreading lower to a distracting area she'd rather not think about at work. Since last night, she'd replayed their kiss over and over. Gotten herself off countless times with her hands, her vibrator, and her fantasies—each more depraved than the last. In every one, she hadn't allowed Tom or anything else to stop them from fucking all night long.

Then at some point she'd conjured up something she'd only read about in the dark of night as she lay in her bed. A ménage à trois. Her between two men. And not just any men.

Nick and Jaxon.

Her pussy contracted in the first stirring of orgasm as she recalled her fantasy of them torturing her naked and defenseless body with their tongues, lips, and teeth.

She blinked away the porno playing in her head and took a tentative sip of her coffee, its bitter taste cannonballing her back to reality.

To keep her mind off sex, she took the opportunity to check out his office. Not surprisingly, it was one of the biggest in the firm. While not a corner office, the sunlight brightened the space, and the cherry wood and chrome furniture gave the room a modern feel. His degrees from the University of Michigan and a couple of framed magazine covers he'd graced hung on the mocha-tinted walls.

She had laminated copies of those same covers in a file back at her apartment.

"Of course it's on your end," Nick said, taking his seat behind the desk. "We have nothing to gain from leaking that information. I expect you to plug the leak or I'm going to speak with my friend the attorney general about the inexcusable actions of your men."

He hung up, shaking his head and swearing under his breath. "I knew it would happen. The media jumped on the kink bandwagon so quickly that I haven't had the chance to prepare a counter campaign."

She pulled up the local news on the Internet. The headline read "A Different Shade of Marriage," with a big picture of a popular leather store that offered products such as whips, floggers, masks, and clothes for the metro-Detroit BDSM community. "Couldn't you hold a press conference? Steer the media away from the whips and chains angle?"

"It would be like adding fuel to a fire. We have to find another suspect." He frowned and clenched his fist, drawing attention to his nails, which were bitten down to the quick. "If we can find someone else who wanted her dead, we could at least get the media off his back." He sighed, rubbing his temples. "But to tell you the truth, I don't know why anyone would want her dead. She was the sweetest woman I'd ever known."

His eyes went glassy, as if he held back tears. It occurred to her he'd known Alyssa for several years. This loss was personal. It wasn't only about saving his friend but finding the true murderer of his other friend.

"Maybe someone set the crime scene to frame Jaxon for the murder," she offered.

"Would you like to see the photos? If not, I completely understand. They're even more graphic than the one you saw at the police station." He lifted a large manila envelope and out slid the photos face down into a pile on his desk.

Prepared for this possibility, she'd taken a pill this morning. "I'll be fine."

She lifted the top picture and flipped it over, telling herself the woman in the photo was a stranger. Not Alyssa Deveroux. Not Jaxon's wife or Nick's friend.

She examined the photo with detached interest. It was a close-up of the victim on her back, her eyes closed and smeared with blood. Then she picked up another picture, this one of her on her stomach. The fingers and toes were purple. Premorbid loss of circulation or postmorbid pooling of blood?

Kate peered closer. "These thin lines were made from a single-tail, but these other welts are thicker." She lowered the photo to the desk and pushed it closer to Nick, pointing to red marks on the back of Alyssa's thighs. "He probably used a cane."

Nick's brows furrowed, creating deep lines in his forehead. "I'm not sure I know what that is."

It didn't surprise her. He didn't play in the BDSM community, and he wasn't exactly the prime target for erotica.

"I have a book I can bring in that might help you understand a little more about BDSM and the types of equipment used. Would that help?" Her face flushed hot. "Or you could look it up online," she added nonchalantly. *Like she had. She'd found all sorts of information about kink on the Internet—even pictures.*

She didn't have anything to be embarrassed about. As evidenced by his friendship with Jaxon, Nick didn't seem to have any sexual hang-ups when it came to the alternative sexual lifestyle.

"I'd appreciate it," he said softly, making her feel more comfortable for suggesting it. "Yes, by all means, bring in the book." He handed her another photo. "What else can you identify from the pictures?"

Something in the photos nagged at her. She was missing something.

When she was a child, she and her father used to play chess. For years she'd blamed her losses on her young age and lack of experience until, one day, her father told her to look at the entire board rather than a single area.

On a hunch, she laid out several of the photos at once, looking at them as a whole rather than piece by piece. And that's when she noticed it. "Thirteen."

"Excuse me?"

Nick watched her intently. "Thirteen whip marks. Thirteen welts. Thirteen cuts. And although it's difficult to tell from the photos, I'm guessing thirteen stab wounds."

They didn't know what it meant, but it had to be a clue. Hopefully, a clue that would lead them away from Jaxon and to the real killer.

"You're amazing," he said with awe.

She shrugged. "In my teens, I went through a dark period where I studied books about serial murderers, satanic cults, and..." His eyebrows shot up. "You think I'm strange."

"Yes. But in a good way. You'll make an excellent attorney, and, despite your protests, I think you'd be well-suited as a criminal defense attorney or, God forbid, a prosecutor."

"You barely know me."

"I know enough. I've been doing this for eleven years, and I've met thousands of lawyers in that time. Not one of them could sit down with a crime photo like I gave you and hone in on such a significant detail in such a short amount of time. In fact, most couldn't stomach a photo like that at all. You're unique, Kate."

"Thank you."

For the first time, she believed she'd have a future at this law firm. By this time next year, she could have her own office. No more uncertainty. A steady paycheck. Job security. Stability.

Everything she'd ever wanted.

Nick leaned back. "What else do you notice in the pictures?"

The killer had left thirteen shallow cuts that weren't made by any traditional BDSM tool, but she recognized the source all the same. Her own father had used the knife every time they'd cleaned their deer after a hunt.

"He used a Buck 110 Folding Hunter Knife to make the cuts and stab wounds."

Nick's jaw slackened. "How could you know that?"

Her hands trembled as she remembered. "I used to go hunting as a kid. This knife is excellent for skinning an animal. It also has a unique angle you can find only with this knife."

"If we can track down who bought this knife, we could find the killer?"

She shook her head, sorry to erase the hope that had flickered in his eyes. "No. It's a common knife. They sell thousands."

"Too bad." His shoulders dropped. "Anything else jump out at you?"

She looked again, focusing on the less obvious. "Bruises. Judging by the yellowing, I'd say they're a few days old." Had Jaxon made these marks as they played? "Shit."

Nick raised a brow. "That's the first time I've heard you swear."

She shrugged. She used to swear like a drunken sailor in a whorehouse, but Nick knew her only as Kate Martin. "Now that we've shared our favorite flavors of ice cream, what's a little profanity among friends?"

"Right. Friends." He gestured with his hand for her to continue. "What was the reason for your expletive?"

"The bruising could help the prosecution build a case that the murder was an escalation of abuse."

"He's wealthy," Nick added, joining Kate in anticipating the prosecution's theories of motivation. "He could've hired someone to kill her."

She closed her eyes and saw it play out like a movie in her mind. Jaxon sitting in a dark, upscale steakhouse with a hired hit man. Eating a steak and drinking bourbon as he calmly instructed the man on how to tie up a woman and torture her to death.

Her gut churned. Something didn't fit with that scenario. "The killer has to be part of the kink scene. Whoever did it knew what he was doing. A single-tail isn't an easy weapon to handle. This was personal to the killer. Thirteen cuts. Thirteen lines from the whip. Thirteen welts. The number means something to him. And unless he drugged her, she had to trust him enough to tie her up. Which means it's probable she was having an affair."

Nick swept up all the photos and tossed them back in the envelope. He dropped it on the desk and sat back in his chair, slightly rocking, his head tilted up toward the ceiling.

"What are you thinking?" she asked.

He didn't answer her for a moment. When he did, she saw the stress of the situation in his tired eyes. "If we don't find the real killer, they're going to put Jaxon away for the crime."

She liked to believe innocent people didn't go to prison, but she'd read the statistics in criminal law class.

Up to 5 percent of the people in prison were innocent. Thousands of men and women were convicted each year for a crime they didn't commit. She couldn't say with 100 percent certainty Jaxon was innocent. But if Nick believed it, she'd hesitate on believing otherwise.

"So what do we do?"

"We do our job." He gave her a small smile. "Welcome to the practice of criminal law."

Chapter Eight

THERE WAS AN urgent knock on the door to Nick's office before it opened a crack. "Mr. Trenton? We have a situation that requires your immediate attention." Lisa, his mousy secretary, poked her head into the room. "Mr. Deveroux is here to see you, but the press has blocked his entrance inside."

Nick swore under his breath as he shot to his feet. "Damn it. Call security and tell them to do their fucking job or I'll make sure they don't have one by the end of the day." He unrolled his sleeves, snatched his suit jacket from his chair, and slipped it on. Back into professional mode. "Ms. Martin, come with me."

She followed him down the hall, curious how he'd handle the situation. In her experience, reporters rarely listened to reason. They had a job to do, and nothing short of arrest would keep them from doing it.

While the Society of Professional Journalists maintained a Code of Ethics, rarely had she met a member of the media who adhered to those standards. Their bosses didn't give a shit about ethics, so long as they got the story and didn't get sued for defamation. False and misleading information was reported all the time, but since the injured party had to prove the extent of the reporter's knowledge of the falsity or careless disregard for the truth rather than mere negligence, lawsuits were rarely won against the media. The reporters usually got away with a slap on the wrist.

She was certain there were decent reporters out there.

She'd just never met one.

When they got to the lobby, she saw three reporters with their backs against the glass doors, holding out microphones to a surrounded Jaxon. He'd have to use force to escape. Exactly what they wanted him to do.

Despite the chaos of the situation, the sight of him stole her breath away. Dressed in a navy suit, his crisp, white shirt unbuttoned at the neck and no tie, Jaxon exuded the classic handsomeness of her favorite old-time movie stars: Cary Grant and Jimmy Stewart. Since yesterday he'd shaven, leaving behind smooth, olive skin, which accentuated his chiseled, high cheekbones and the scar bisecting his thick, dark brow. He raked his fingers through the tamed curls of his raven hair, hair that had that sexy just-rolled-out-of-bed look that people spent fortunes on in Hollywood. But he wasn't perfect. From this angle, she could see his nose was slightly uneven, with a small bump on the bridge, as if at some point he had broken it. To her, the imperfection managed to symbolize his rugged masculinity.

When the commotion escalated, Kate tore her gaze away from him and scanned the area, stopping on the glass doors to the firm.

"Nick!" she shouted, pointing to the doors and alerting him to her plan. She raced to the doors and threw one open wide. Three male reporters stumbled backward into the office, giving Nick an opportunity to elbow his way through the frenzy.

Rachel Dawson, a popular Detroit morning newscaster known for her solid reporting, long raven hair, and ample-sized chest, shoved through the crowd and thrust her microphone directly under Jaxon's chin, almost daring him to push her away. "Mr. Deveroux! Could you tell us why you enjoyed beating your wife?"

"Don't say a word, Jaxon." Nick grasped him by the neck of his shirt and ushered him through the crowd. When they got inside, Nick stretched out his arms in front of Jaxon like a professional bodyguard and said, "My client will not answer any of your questions. This is private property, and I'm going to ask you all to leave or I'll call the police."

One of the reporters in the lobby smirked and pointed his phone at Nick, no doubt set to record audio. "Mr. Trenton, are you also a BDSM master?"

Nicks hands curled into fists, but he remained in control. Kate heard the voices of the building's security guards ordering the reporters to disperse.

Some of the media heeded the warnings, but Rachel wasn't as smart. Rather than follow the others, she suddenly broke away from the crowd and barreled into the room. "What is your response to attorney general candidate Mason Ford's call for a grand jury investigation into the murder of your wife?" she asked Jaxon.

Jaxon blanched and wobbled on his feet. Although he topped her by almost a foot, she repaid the favor from yesterday and slid an arm around his waist to keep him upright.

Nick stalked to Rachel. "I would think you'd know better, Ms. Dawson. That's nothing more than campaign rhetoric. Now, I believe I told you to leave this property. Don't make me ask you again."

The pretty reporter blinked but didn't budge. "You can't make me leave. This is private property open to the public, and I have every right to be here."

"You are inside the office, and I've asked you to leave," Nick said with a tone of dangerous restraint. "You do not have the right to remain. As for being inside the building, the owner has already been contacted and you were causing a public nuisance. I'm sure every firm on this floor would back me up in saying you've interrupted business. Furthermore, you are not here for the purpose of doing business with one of the tenants. You've trailed my client, a private citizen, and invaded his privacy rights. I'm not sure your boss wants the wrath of this firm raining down on his station. Now get out."

"Thanks for the sound bite, Trenton. Make sure you catch the news at noon." Rachel blew him a kiss and strutted away.

Jaxon released a long exhale. "It hasn't stopped. Somehow the media found out where I'm staying, and they've been camped out in front of the hotel twenty-four-seven. My phone hasn't stopped ringing. My *unlisted* cell, I might add. I lost my wife and now I've lost my privacy. No one cares about getting my side of the story. They just want to win the ratings for their time slot. Alyssa chaired committees to raise money for victims of sexual abuse. She donated blood and raised awareness of the bone marrow registry. But now she's forever memorialized as a brainwashed victim of domestic violence."

Nick cocked a brow at her, and she realized she still had her arm around their client. Embarrassed, Kate stepped away from him.

Her boss patted Jaxon on the back and, with a jab of his chin, motioned to them to return to his office. "We're doing everything we can. I've got calls into a couple of psychiatrists who specialize in sex therapy and BDSM. Hopefully, if we convince the media to interview them, it'll change the community's perception. The problem is people are scared of what they don't know."

"What about the coroner?" Jaxon asked as they proceeded down the hallway. "Won't he be able to find evidence to clear me?"

Kate and Nick's gazes collided as she recalled their earlier conversation over the photos. "Our county has a medical examiner. And, of course, it's possible he'll find a fingerprint or DNA evidence that will help lead the police to the real killer. But her death wasn't committed in the heat of passion. Whoever did it was meticulous. Which means the chance he made a mistake and left behind evidence is reduced."

With a file in her hands, Lisa stepped out of Nick's office, her eyes widening at the sight of an approaching Jaxon.

If the firm's own employees were apprehensive in his presence, how would they ever convince the general public of his innocence? Or was it simply the knowledge that the man beat his wife for pleasure that unnerved them?

Lisa swallowed hard. "Mr. Trenton, I placed the fax you've been waiting for on your desk."

"Thank you, Lisa," Nick said. "Please hold my calls while I'm with Mr. Deveroux."

"Of course, sir." Averting her eyes, she angled her body toward Jaxon and bounced from foot to foot. "Can I get you a refreshment? We have bottled water, juice, and a variety of pop."

"No, thank you."

The secretary blew out a huge breath and bolted back to her desk.

Nick ushered Kate and Jaxon inside his office. They sat in silence as Nick perused the fax.

When he lifted his head, she read the agony on his face. "This is from the medical examiner's office. He's preliminarily ruling Alyssa's death a homicide with cause of death asphyxiation by ligature strangulation. Do you want me explain the report to you or would you prefer to read it yourself?"

Blanching, Jaxon started to reach for the fax but then dropped his hand to Nick's desk. "Did she…suffer?"

She wanted to hug him close, massage her fingers into his thick hair, and ease his torment. Judging by the photos alone, Alyssa had endured a horrific death, and it hadn't come quickly.

At least Kate's father had died instantly. Only the people he'd left behind had suffered.

"I'm sorry, Jaxon." Nick's skin had taken on a slightly green tinge. "According to the medical examiner, the killer must have first tried to get her to strangle herself. The way he'd bound her, if she'd tired and dropped her head forward or passed out, the rope would have strangled her. As it was, it severely decreased her oxygen levels. But it was the addition of the collar that cut off her ability to breathe. Based on the blood evidence, the stab wounds were inflicted postmortem. Most of the bruising was determined to have been caused within an hour of her death, but the medical examiner did note prior bruising on her posterior."

Jaxon breathed heavily as he processed the information. "I don't understand why I'm still a suspect. I have an alibi."

"They might believe you hired someone to do it for you," Kate said, curling her fingers into her pants to keep from touching him. "The police will subpoena your bank records to look for any large or unusual withdrawals of money."

"They can look all they want. They're not going to find anything." Jaxon stared at her almost as if he could read her thoughts. As if he knew how much she wanted to help him. Please him.

What would he think about her if he discovered she'd fantasized about fucking him and Nick at the same time?

Nick's baritone voice drew Jaxon's gaze away from her, and she realized she'd been holding her breath. "It doesn't matter. If they can't get you for murder, they'll charge you with battery based on the fact you were Alyssa's Dom. The newspapers are filled with letters from outraged women's rights organizations crying for justice and swinging support to Ford in the upcoming election. The pressure is on Savage to file charges or he's out of office come November. Right now, you're political fodder. They're out for blood. Your blood. It's my job to keep you from making it easy on them, and, if they arrest you, I've got to find reasonable doubt. Because you know the whole fucking 'innocent until proven guilty' phrase you're always hearing about? Well, it doesn't work that way. Occam's razor: the simplest explanation is usually true." Nick leaned forward, planting both hands on his desk. "I have to ask. Were you and Alyssa having marital problems?"

Other than a muscle jumping in Jaxon's jaw, he went completely still. "We shared a house, but not a bed. The day I left for Chicago, I asked for a divorce." He spoke softly, as if each word pained him, and she heard what he didn't say.

What if…?

"Why didn't you tell me?" Nick asked gently.

"What was I going to say? Alyssa and I haven't made love in eighteen months? That I wasn't enough for her sexually, and so she had to go out and hire a professional Dominatrix to beat her so she could have an orgasm? That I'd failed both as her Dom and her husband?"

Nick held out his hands. "How the hell am I supposed to keep you out of jail if you're keeping things from me?"

After a brief silence, Jaxon spoke so quietly it startled her. "You never asked."

"I'm supposed to ask if you were fucking your wife?" Nick asked.

"No. Not that." Jaxon twisted his thick, gold wedding band. "You never asked if I killed her."

"I don't need to." Nick jumped to his feet and circled his desk to stand by his friend. "The man I've known since college, who made me crash on his couch because I was too drunk to drive, that guy is not a murderer. I didn't need to ask because I know you didn't do it." He squeezed Jaxon's shoulder, providing the comfort Kate didn't have the right to give.

A twinge of envy stabbed her chest. In some ways, she felt like an intruder as she witnessed the bond between these two men. If she was in Jaxon's situation, would she have anyone to watch her back? Tom? Hannah? Caden? Or would they all disappear like the last time she'd needed the unconditional support of a friend?

Jaxon thumped Nick's arm a couple of times, thanking his best friend without speaking the words. "Couldn't we hire our own detective? Maybe he could come up with something different than the police."

Antsy, she rolled a pen in her hands. "The killer is one of you. A kinkster. Whoever does the investigating also has to be part of the scene; otherwise he'll never get anyone to talk. Do you know anyone in the community who could help?"

"You mean a private investigator?" Jaxon frowned. "Not that I know of. Besides, it's been a few years since I've visited our club. When Alyssa and I agreed to separate, we decided she would use our membership at Benediction since she needed it more. That's where she met her Dominatrix twice a week for her sessions."

Kate's mind flew to a hot, sweaty place she'd only read about. Within it lay their answer. A local sex club filled with people who could wield a single-tail whip. People who may have spoken with Alyssa or had knowledge of who'd want her dead.

She swallowed her apprehension. "I have an idea. It's unconventional, but I can't think of another way."

"Anything," Jaxon said.

Nervous energy forced her to her feet. She paced the length of the office, rubbing the gold cross hanging on her necklace between her fingers. The irony of it bubbled in her stomach, almost making her laugh. Not that an atheist wearing a cross wasn't ironic enough. "Jaxon needs to go to the club and get back into the scene. They'll talk to him."

A frowning Nick tilted his head. "Won't it seem odd for him to go to a sex club so soon after the murder of Alyssa?"

Playing with his wedding band again, Jaxon stared at her, understanding evident in his eyes. "Some people may take it as a sign of guilt. Others may see it as a way to regain control over an uncontrollable situation."

Nick reclined in his chair and crossed his arms. "So you just go and ask questions? I don't see how that would work."

"It wouldn't," she said. "He needs a reason to be there." Stopping in front of Nick, she placed her hand on his solid shoulder. "Me. I'd go with him as his sub."

He shot to his feet, his eyes blazing with dissent. "No. Absolutely not. As a member of Jaxon's legal team, you cannot have a personal relationship, even a pretend one. It's unethical."

"I'll wear a mask," she said in a quiet voice, attempting to soothe the wild beast she'd uncaged. "No one will know."

"*I'll* know." He turned her to him and placed his hands on her shoulders. "It's my role as your supervisor to ensure you don't violate the Michigan Rules of Professional Conduct."

If Jaxon had not been in the room, she would have accused Nick of allowing his personal feelings for her to get in the way of the case. "Going undercover as Jaxon's submissive doesn't violate the code. There isn't even an explicit rule against having sex with a client."

"That may be, but I've known a few attorneys censured by the Michigan Bar for sleeping with a client. At this point, it would ruin your career. Besides, you're not a cop or a private investigator. It isn't your job to play Nancy Drew."

"You're right. But an attorney acts as an advocate for his client and what better way to advocate for Jaxon than to find Alyssa's real killer to prove his innocence?"

"That's stretching the definition of advocate a bit, don't you think?" He lowered his voice. "Do you realize what kinds of things go on at that club?"

She couldn't hold back her smile. *He was jealous.* "Not exactly. But I can use my imagination."

He tucked a stray hair behind her ear. "This isn't funny. You're too young, and it's too dangerous."

"She's older than I was when Alyssa took me to my first play party," Jaxon offered from his seat.

Nick dropped his hands to his side and stepped back from her, his gaze never leaving her face. He shook his head as if coming out of a trance and crossed to Jaxon. "I only know what you've told me about Benediction. Are you willing to take an innocent girl like Kate there? You can't possibly prepare her for whom and what she'll encounter." He didn't wait for Jaxon to answer before whipping his attention back to Kate. "And you. Are you ready to bow naked before your master where anyone and everyone can see you?"

"Nick is right, although not about the master part," Jaxon said calmly, rising from his chair. "While your idea has merit, we can't subject you to a lifestyle you know nothing about or even want."

She stomped to stand between Nick and Jaxon. "I'm not innocent and I'm not naïve. I understand what I'll have to do as Jaxon's submissive, and I want to do it. I need to do it."

Nick paused. "Give me a week to come up with another plan. Another way."

"We don't have a week," she reminded him. "I've been through this before. The prosecution will twist every piece of evidence to make their case, and when they discover they're wrong, they'll cover their political asses rather than admit they made a mistake."

Nick startled. "What do you mean you've been through this before?

"I...You know I'm right," she said, ignoring the question. "I admit I haven't been to a sex club. I may have read some romantic fiction about sexy billionaire men with emotional issues who call themselves Doms, but I've also done quite a bit of research online about BDSM."

Nick folded his arms across his chest. "I don't care if you've written an entire dissertation on BDSM. I'm not jeopardizing your safety."

"Even for your best friend?" she asked, knowing it was a low blow.

Jaxon edged closer to her, boxing her in between the two men. "I'll be with her the entire time, Nick. I won't allow anyone to touch her, and I won't push her to do anything she doesn't want. You can trust me with her."

"It's not about trust," Nick said softly.

"Then what is it about?" asked Jaxon.

Heady warmth unfurled in her chest and her pulse quickened as she fell to her knees and bowed her head. "Sir, may I please attend Benediction as Jaxon's submissive?"

The men went completely silent. Not a breath could be heard. She almost felt their ravenous gazes on her. Would this prove to them she'd play a convincing submissive?

Nick tilted up her chin and looked at her with a mix of heat and sadness. "Yes."

Chapter Nine

Twelve Days to Elections...

"I APPRECIATE YOU coming with me to the house," Jaxon said as they stood on the porch of his substantial home. Heck, she could fit ten of her mama's double-wides in this place.

The professional crime scene cleaning company had given the all clear for Jaxon to return home, and since time was of the essence, he'd agreed to begin her training this morning in his personal dungeon.

She followed him through the front door, her voice echoing in the entryway. "It's not a problem. I understand how difficult it is for you."

He smiled, but it didn't meet his eyes. "You know most people who say something like that really don't know how difficult it is. It's like when people ask you how you're doing; they don't expect an answer other than fine. When you ask, I believe you really want to hear the truth."

"That's because I do." Their gazes locked, knocking her off-kilter.

Jaxon appeared years younger than thirty-five, dressed in a relaxed pair of faded jeans and a simple black T-shirt that spread tightly across his broad chest. The suits she'd previously seen him in had hidden the masculine beauty underneath. He wasn't built like a rich businessman. At least none she'd ever known. If she'd met him on the street, she'd peg him for a construction worker. Tall, lean, broad-shouldered. And she could drown in his expressive eyes.

"Your house is beautiful," she managed to say, heading toward the winding staircase. "Umm...we should probably get started."

A stoic blank slate replaced his smile. There was an air of duty in his stride as he climbed the steps to the second level of the house. He hadn't spoken a word about returning to the scene of the crime, but how could it not haunt him? The scent of bleach was so thick it stung her nose and brought tears to her eyes. A tangible reminder of the violence it had scrubbed clean. But the stench of blood and death lingered in the memory, which neither bleach nor time could erase.

When they reached the landing, Jaxon stopped, his body taut with tension and his hands fisted at his side, showing he wasn't quite as immune as he pretended to be. Instinctively, she rested her hand on his shoulder blade in an effort to comfort him. The hard muscles of his back rippled under her fingers.

"We don't have to do this here," she said.

They could have met at the law firm or in his hotel room, but he'd insisted on using his dungeon to give her the full effect.

He didn't respond for what felt like minutes. Then he murmured, "Yes, we do," and proceeded down the hallway.

The walls were decorated with bright, colorful paintings of landscapes. She didn't claim to know the first thing about art, but this felt sterile and impersonal.

In the trailer where she'd grown up, the walls were covered with photographs of her parents throughout their marriage and every class photo of Kate through her freshman year of high school.

After her father had died, it had pained her to roam the halls with the constant memory of what she'd lost. But eventually, she was grateful she had documentation of a happier time. She clung to those memories like a toddler to a security blanket. The photos had given her the strength to find new dreams. She may have been victimized, but it didn't mean she had to become a victim.

They passed several closed doors before Jaxon took out a key and unlocked one. She steeled herself, having seen a sex dungeon only on the news—a tiny, dark, decrepit basement with a couple of menacing whips hanging on the wall—and she was pretty sure the descriptions in the erotica she'd read were made up to sound sexier to the readers.

This dungeon was on the second floor of the house, and, from what she'd witnessed so far, there wasn't anything dark about his home. Or, surprisingly, the man himself.

Weren't Dominants supposed to be all broody and intense? Jaxon didn't fit the mold she'd envisioned of a man who enjoyed the BDSM lifestyle. Yes, he'd just lost his wife and there was somberness in him, but even so, she'd never call him dark.

He was surprisingly…normal.

He pushed open the door and then flicked on the lights. His body blocked the view of the room, but the clean scent of pine greeted her. He strode inside, pivoted, and, with a crook of his finger, beckoned her to cross the threshold as if offering her a taste of forbidden fruit. She worried her lip between her teeth, her entire body trembling. Exactly why she wasn't certain. But she did know, once she stepped inside, her life would never be the same.

The room looked nothing like she'd imagined. Rich caramel-colored hardwood floors warmed the space, as did the crème-colored walls. Except for the gorgeous wooden St. Andrew's cross and what, at first glance, appeared to be a gynecological examination table, she could find the remaining furniture in any living room. A chaise lounge made of brown leather. A round, cushioned chair. A long couch with throw pillows. The beautiful armoire in the far corner of the room drew her attention, and she moved closer to admire it. She fingered its intricate flower etching. "When I thought of a dungeon, I thought of…well, a dungeon."

"I prefer to call it a playroom." He stalked across the floor until he stood immediately behind her, so close his warm breath caressed her neck. "What were you picturing? Chains attached to stone walls, concrete floors, and instruments of torture?"

She shivered. The scent of pine intensified, and she realized the entire room smelled like Jaxon. "I wasn't sure what to expect, but yes, I'd thought you would have whips and crops."

"Don't worry. I've got plenty of them, but I prefer to keep them organized in the armoire you're admiring." She stilled, the heat of his chest on her back. "I built it with my own two hands. Same as the St. Andrew's cross. Gives me an extra thrill to know something so innocent can cause so much pleasure. So much pain." His hair tickled her cheek as he whispered, "Go on and open it. You know you want to."

Her stomach clenching, she gripped the armoire doors but couldn't force herself to see what waited for her inside. Why was she afraid?

She trusted he wouldn't do anything she didn't want. The problem was…she didn't know what she wanted.

Liar.

The problem wasn't that she didn't know what she wanted. The problem was she shouldn't want it. Especially not with Jaxon.

Curiosity won. Lightheaded from the anticipation, she tugged open the doors, her heart galloping faster than a racehorse.

Her eyes scanned from top to bottom. Three shelves. Several iron hooks bolted into the back of the armoire.

All empty.

She spun and pushed against Jaxon's chest. "You played me."

A slight smirk formed on his face. "A little. Just a kindergarten version of a mind fuck." He stepped back, and the smile melted away like an ice cube on an August day. "Actually, the police confiscated all of it for testing. To see if it contained evidence of…"

She itched to cradle his cheek in her hand. Instead, she closed the doors to conceal the memory of what he'd lost and whispered, "The armoire is beautiful. You're very talented."

His face morphed into stone once again. Unreadable.

He trudged to the couch. "The first lesson I need to teach you is how to stand and present yourself. Did you ever sing in a choir?"

Thrown by the sudden chill in the room as well as the change in topic, she faltered. "Sure, my freshman year of high school." Before her father died, she'd loved to sing. Had even beaten out a couple of the older students for a solo in the Christmas concert. By the end of the school year, she hadn't bothered to show up for class.

"Do you remember how you were expected to stand?"

She joined him in the center of the room in front of the U-shaped couch. "Shoulders dropped and pushed back, feet spread apart, don't lock the knees."

"Do it." He issued his command quietly, but there was a harsh edge to it that she'd never heard from him. As she complied with his bidding, tendrils of heat swirled in her core and her breasts grew heavy with want. She waited for further instructions, praying he wouldn't notice her hardened nipples pressing against her bra. "Now bow your head slightly, keeping your gaze on the floor in front of you. If we're in a scene, I'd expect you to clasp your hands behind your back, but while we're exploring the club, feel free to keep them relaxed at your side."

She slowed her breathing. "Will I have to be naked?"

He chuckled. "No. The first time we go, you can wear a black skirt, the shorter the better. Do you own a corset?"

"Yes." She'd bought the corset and matching panties to surprise Tom but had never found the courage to wear them.

"Wear the corset for your top. Comfortable shoes since you may be on your feet for a long period of time. Hair down." He moved behind her. His hand brushed the side of her neck, his fingers playing with one of her blond curls. "You have beautiful hair."

Her lids fluttered shut. "Th-Thank you."

"Have you ever been tied up? Bound during sex?"

"No," she whispered. She couldn't speak any louder.

His cheek's stubble rubbed against her neck. "Never had a lover pull your hair or bite you or spank you with the back of his hand?"

Her pussy quivered, liquid desire dampening her panties. *Was it possible to climax simply from listening to his voice?*

"Do you fantasize about it? Tell me the truth. I'm not going to judge you. You're always safe with me."

Safe? She was two seconds away from forgetting she had a boyfriend. To regain control, she broke from her submissive position and turned. "Who hasn't fantasized about it?"

He frowned. "When we are in a scene, you will refer to me as 'Jax.' Understood?"

The disappointment on his face sent a sharp pang in her chest. "Yes, Jax."

He moved closer. Close enough for her to feel the erection hidden by his jeans. "What is Kate short for? Katherine? Kathleen?"

"Katerina," she answered without thinking. No one in Detroit knew her as anything other than Kate since she'd legally changed it at eighteen. How had he made her forget to lie?

"Like you, beautiful and unique. When I use it, you'll know we're in a scene." She nodded, unable to speak. He cradled her head in his hands. "Now tell me the truth. Do you fantasize about a man taking control over you sexually?"

She couldn't look away from his brown eyes. Couldn't resist answering. "Yes."

He arched a brow. "Yes, who?"

"Yes, Jax."

"Have you ever used nipple clamps?"

They tingled at the suggestion. "No, Jax."

"A vibrator?"

The lawyer in her wanted to challenge the relevance of these questions, but like she was under his spell, she felt compelled to answer. "Yes, Jax."

"What kind?"

Kind? Was he kidding? "I don't understand."

"You are an innocent, aren't you? Clitoral, vaginal, anal, dual?"

Dual? Her pussy throbbed. She'd rub her thighs together if it wouldn't clue him in as to how much his questions aroused her. It had been a long time since she'd been an innocent, but these questions made her feel like one. "Um…It's just your average purple vibrator." She added teasingly, "It's shaped like a Popsicle…Jax."

"I like grape Popsicles." He licked his lips. Was he imagining its taste? Or hers? "Have you ever been handcuffed?"

A memory sparked and her chest tightened. The phantom sensation of steel pinched her wrists. She tried breathing through her nose like Nick had suggested at the police station. "Not for sexual purposes."

"Why then?"

She tried to pull away, but his hands held her firm in his grasp. "I don't…I don't talk about that."

Soothing her, he drifted the back of his hand over her cheek. "It's all right. You don't have to tell me…yet."

Her throat grew dry, and she licked her parched lips. Anger rose to the surface at the suggestion that he'd expect her to reveal her past. She didn't talk about it with anyone. Not even Tom. "Why all these questions? I thought you were going to train me."

"Training isn't only physical. It's mental. Emotional. Even spiritual. At Benediction, it won't be good enough to *pretend* you're my submissive. You will have to *be my submissive*. In every way. You've indicated you have some knowledge of BDSM, and so you understand it's a power exchange. A negotiation of parameters. Those items you may not be ready for at the moment but are not completely off the table are your soft limits. I may push those boundaries at some point. But I will not challenge you on your hard limits. You will entrust me with power over your body, and I will honor your wishes. Keep you safe. My pleasure derives from yours. While it would arouse me to parade you naked through the club wearing nothing but jewelry dangling from your nipples, I will only choose scenes I know will please you. These questions may seem personal to you, but soon I'll see and touch the most intimate parts of your body. Parts you may not have even explored. As my sub, you'll have to trust that everything I say and do has a purpose, even if you're not aware of what it is. If you can't accept my terms, we'll find another way to prove my innocence."

"But I'm not submissive."

Was she? His words penetrated those protective boundaries she'd carefully constructed and accessed her most personal desires as if he'd plucked them out of her conscience. The ones she thought about at night when she lay alone underneath the cool sheets and explored her own body, picturing herself tied spread-eagle to a bed by a stranger. Helpless. Defenseless. Empowered. But those were her fantasies. In reality, she wouldn't trust anyone with that amount of power over her.

"Don't lie to me or yourself. Any Dom worth a damn would see your submissiveness from miles away. Believe me, I was drawn to you from the moment you slid into the interrogation room, so desperate to please your boss, you wouldn't even ask for a chair."

Her body shuddered at the idea that this man desired *her*.

"No bodily fluids. No needles or permanent marks. And no bondage. Those are my hard limits."

"If I hold you down with my hands…?"

"Maybe," she said with a sigh, the fire between her legs burning brighter at the thought. "It's a soft limit." There was a limit to the amount of control she'd give. She wouldn't place herself in a position where she'd be completely helpless, no matter what she fantasized.

"You think you know what you're going to see at Benediction, but I can't possibly prepare you for the seductive debaucheries on display. When Cole DeMarco opened his home to the kink community fifteen years ago after the state closed the public club he belonged to, he wanted a place where people could safely participate in whatever their kinky hearts desired. It's not solely a BDSM club. It's a den of iniquity. As long as you're over eighteen and pay the membership fee, all your darkest fantasies can be brought to life. Whether it involves bondage, sadomasochism, voyeurism, exhibitionism, roleplaying, or simply a foot massage, nothing is off limits." His hair caressed her cheek as he whispered in her ear, "Tell me. What's your desire?"

How could she vocalize her desires when she didn't know how to put them into words? Her fantasies were just that: fantasies. The fact that her pussy swelled at the thought of being tied down and bound with rope didn't mean she'd actually enjoy it. "My only desire is to find Alyssa's killer," she whispered in return.

He lifted his head and a million emotions passed through his eyes before they settled on something akin to regret. Whether it was for Alyssa or because she hadn't answered his question, she didn't know. "Benediction recognizes 'red' as the club's universal safe word. Red means everything stops. You use 'yellow' when you want to slow down and we'll talk. Green means you're good to go. But if you want, you can pick a safe word in addition to red. Something you'll remember."

"Gunshot," she said automatically.

His palm drifted down her cheek to her shoulder. "I'm not the only one who's been touched by violence, am I?"

"Hasn't everyone?" she countered, shivering, thrown by how in tune he was with her thoughts. Her emotions. Her body.

His brown eyes smoldered, and, for the first time, she sensed darkness in him. "No. Not like we have. Looking into your eyes is like looking in a mirror. Maybe that's why..." He smoothed the callused pads of his fingers along her collarbone, leaving goose bumps in their wake and beading her nipples.

Was this another part of her training? Because it felt real. Realer than the artwork hanging on the walls of his home. This felt dangerous. Exciting. Alive. She felt way too much for this man. A man suspected of murdering his wife. A man who wasn't Tom. A man who was her client.

Yet despite the possible ethical and legal ramifications of becoming sexually involved with him, she silently willed those fingers to move south, needing to feel those calluses abrade her aching nipples. But the Dom in him was obviously on his own timetable because he continued to skim his fingers across the length of her collarbone. A needy, breathy moan escaped from her throat, darkening his eyes to onyx. With one hand splayed low on her back, he pressed her against the ridge of his erection, proving in the most delicious way that this attraction wasn't one-sided. His head dipped lower, his lips edged closer, and his fingers drifted down the upper swell of her breast, so close to her nipple she thought she'd go insane if he didn't make contact soon.

She wanted him.

Consequences be damned.

Chapter Ten

His lips hovered over hers, his breath sweet and warm. They hadn't even kissed, yet she'd never been so aroused, the walls of her slick pussy fluttering in the hope that Jax would soon fill it with his thick fingers, his tongue, or his cock. Rational thought had fled and been replaced with pure, wanton physical desire.

Until the shrill ringing of a phone broke through the sensual fog, dropping her straight back into reality.

She backed away from him, rubbing her neglected lips. Except for his throat working over a swallow, he didn't move a muscle. His eyes returned to their normal golden brown.

He motioned to her pants. "Are you going to answer?"

Oh. It was *her* phone. She slid the cell from the pocket of her black slacks.

Nick.

Swamped with guilt, she answered. "Hi, Nick. How was trial?"

"We settled. How's your training?"

She tried to sound normal. "Great. Jaxon was just about to take me home. We're ready for Benediction tomorrow night."

He was silent.

"Nick? Are you there?"

"Yeah. Sorry. I got distracted." He cleared his throat. "I'll see you in the morning." The call disconnected.

Had she said something wrong? Had he somehow figured out what he'd interrupted?

"I'll take you home," Jax said. Then, without another word, he left her alone in the playroom.

The ride home wasn't any better. He'd barely spoken other than to ask for directions. It shouldn't bother her. She'd obviously misread their connection. Just because he was attracted to her didn't mean he wanted anything to happen between them other than what was necessary to convince everyone she was his sub. The erotic caresses, the almost kiss, the hard cock against her belly. None of it had meant a damn thing.

Her entire body hummed with the kind of need only an orgasm or two, and not the self-induced kind, would satiate. She glanced at the dashboard clock. Tom should be home from work by now, and she hadn't seen him in a few days. A night with him would remind her of why she loved him, and then she could mentally slot Nick and Jaxon in their proper places as her boss and client. "I've changed my mind. Up at the next light, make a left."

"Where am I taking you, Kate?"

Kate. Not Katerina. Disappointment lanced her chest. She could lie. She didn't owe him anything. "My boyfriend's apartment," she answered honestly.

Bittersweet triumph rocked her off her foundation when his hands tightened on the steering wheel.

"Dating long?" he asked casually.

"Two years." They'd met on campus during her first year of law school when he was in his last year of medical school. Two souls who didn't bother to stop studying for a minute. Their books spread out in front of them as they ate the cafeteria's soggy sandwiches. After seeing each other every day at lunch for a week, he'd started up a conversation with her. He later confessed he'd wanted to ask her out the first day he'd spotted her, but it took him the week to gather his courage. It seemed like a lifetime ago.

He was the first man she'd dated since…well, she'd never actually *dated* before Tom. Smart and stable with his life planned from his residency to retirement in Santa Fe. He'd understood her drive for success and didn't complain when she'd fall asleep on his couch with a law book on her chest. They'd settled into a comfortable routine. At least until she'd begun interning for Nick.

Between school, studying, and work, she'd had no time or energy for dinner and a movie followed by a ten-minute session of missionary-position sex. But as she'd learned a decade ago at age fourteen, sex had nothing to do with love. So what if their sex life was a bit boring?

They loved each other. Supported each other's careers. Shared common interests.

In the scheme of things, the sex wasn't important. They were friends. Yet he knew little of her past. Didn't know her real name. And he had no idea she was planning on going to a sex club as her client's submissive. It was confidential, but even if it wasn't, he'd never approve or understand how far she'd go to prove Jaxon's innocence. After all, he didn't know the truth behind why she'd decided to become an attorney.

Her boyfriend conveniently lived a few blocks from her apartment, but his was spacious and a whole lot nicer than her dump. It was also an extra $600 a month. He'd asked her to move in with him, but she wasn't ready for that kind of commitment.

A minute later, they approached Tom's building. "It's that one. On the right," she said, pointing to the apartment.

He veered the car to the curb in front of the building before placing it in park. She unbuckled and then pivoted to say good-night, but he spoke first. "Your boyfriend... it's serious?" He ran his fingers through his hair. "Forget I asked. It's none of my business."

No, it wasn't. But how she wished it was...

"Good-night, Jaxon."

The inclination to kiss his cheek was overwhelming, and she leaned forward. He stopped her with a firm hand on her shoulder. "Sleep well, Kate."

Tonight he wouldn't allow her to kiss his cheek. Tomorrow he was taking her half naked to a sex club where he might have to touch her most intimate places. Why did she think this plan would work?

Departing his car, she was greeted by the hot, sticky evening air, the kind of air that signaled an imminent rainstorm. When he drove away, she unlocked the front door of Tom's building.

Running up the steps to the third floor, she raked her fingers through her hair, trying to tame it before she pounced on her boyfriend. The high humidity had frizzed her hair into a wild mess. Appropriate since that's how she felt right now.

Jaxon had aroused a storm in her the size of a hurricane. Tom wouldn't know what hit him by the time she was finished with him. She almost hoped she'd find him asleep so she could quietly crawl into bed and slide his boxers down his thighs. He'd awaken with his cock deep in her mouth, and then she'd impale herself on him before he could coax her into their typical missionary sex.

She rapped on his door and waited. When he didn't answer, she figured he was either still at work or asleep. Either way, she'd surprise him. She unlocked his door and slipped inside his dark apartment. After setting her purse on the small table next to the door, she crept across the family room toward the back of the one-bedroom apartment.

The creaking of the bedsprings and Tom's low moan alerted her to his presence. Shit, she'd interrupted him masturbating.

She paused by his closed bedroom door, aroused by his animalistic groans and grunts. Should she make some noise so he'd know she was there? She twisted the doorknob and cracked open the door, wanting a visual to go with the audio before she jumped him. And that's when she heard *her*.

"You like my hot cunt, baby? It's all yours."

With her spine arched, her head thrown back in wild abandon, and her blond curls cascading over her shoulders, Hannah rode a blindfolded Tom.

Frozen in shock, Kate watched the scene, disgusted by their betrayal but, at the same time, aroused by their private dance. Each swirl of Hannah's hips, each perfectly timed upward thrust of Tom's pelvis against her clitoris was to a rhythm only they could hear.

They connected on more than a physical level. Their bodies gleamed with sweat, the scent of sex so thick in the air, it was almost visible.

This wasn't a one-time mistake. Anyone could sense they'd made love countless times in the past.

And if it didn't hurt so damn much to watch, it would have been beautiful.

"Tom! Tom! I'm going to come!" Hannah shouted, her pace increasing.

He gripped the sides of her hips and slammed her down against him. "Come all over my dick!"

For some reason, she felt compelled to wait until they climaxed before she interrupted. Then she clapped, giving them the kudos they deserved. "I'd give it a ten, but I had to take a point off for dramatics."

Hannah squealed in shock, crossing her arms over her chest to hide her breasts while Tom whipped off his blindfold.

"Shit. Kate. What are you doing here?"

"That's rich. What am I doing here? The question is how could you both do this to me?"

Oh God. *She* was the frigid girlfriend Hannah had mentioned in the bar. That her two closest friends had lied to her was bad enough, but the thought of Hannah laughing behind her back sliced her open, leaving her raw and exposed.

Hannah took Tom's hand. "Kate, we didn't mean for this to happen, and the last thing I wanted to do was hurt you."

She refused to waste tears on these two. "Right, because screwing my boyfriend behind my back wouldn't hurt me."

Tom disengaged from Hannah's grip and scrambled out of bed, yanking on a pair of sweats. "Wait, Katie."

"Good-bye, Tom. I hope you're happy with her. You deserve each other. Hannah, stay away from me at work or, I swear, I'll make you pay." She raced out of the apartment, grabbing her purse on the way.

How could she be so stupid? All this time, she'd thought staying with a man as predictable as Tom would keep her safe. But he'd played her for a fool. Apparently, he wasn't the dud in the sack. She was.

The whole situation hurt her head. Her heart raced and she couldn't catch her breath. She needed a pill.

As she trotted down the stairs, Tom shouted her name from a few feet behind her. She didn't want to talk. Didn't want to hear his excuses. There was nothing he could say to make this right. Her trust for him had been based on the man she thought he was, but she'd cared for a mirage.

She flew out the building to the dark street and into a downpour of rain. The single working streetlamp cast Tom's shadow onto the sidewalk. The door banged, and he trudged behind her, breathless and smelling like Hannah.

"Kate, please let me explain," he begged. The hands that had earlier gripped Hannah's hips now cupped her shoulders, swiveling her around to face him.

"There's nothing you can say to make this right. We're done. I don't want to ever see you again," she said, surprising herself with the calm in her voice.

"You don't mean that. I know I messed up, but she threw herself at me. I didn't go out intending to sleep with her."

When his gaze slid to her chest, she looked down. Damn it! Her nipples were visible under her soaked white blouse. She folded her arms across her chest.

Despite the warm air, she was racked with chills, causing her teeth to chatter. "Right. Your dick accidentally fell into her pussy."

He winced. "One night I ran into her at the bar. We just talked. Honestly. We commiserated about how you'd withdrawn from us since starting the internship. We missed you. So we figured we'd keep each other company. As friends. I rarely saw you, and, honestly, I didn't think you'd even notice if I *married* another woman. I may have cheated with Hannah, but you're not innocent either. You cheated on me with Nick."

Her heart sank to her drenched feet. How had he found out about their kiss? "It didn't—"

He spoke over her without giving her a chance to explain. "Yeah, I know there's nothing sexual going on with the two of you, but you're infatuated with him. Obsessed almost. How am I supposed to compete with the perfect Nicholas Trenton? I guess after a while I decided to take myself out of the running."

She held up her hand and twirled in the direction of her apartment, determined to get home before she crumbled. "I can't believe you're blaming me for your cheating."

He ran after her and seized her arm, spinning her back around. "At least let me give you a ride home."

Tired, angry, and confused, all she wanted was to hide under the covers of her warm bed. But she refused to spend another minute with him, even if it meant she'd escape the rain and get to her bed that much quicker. She tried yanking her arm from his firm grasp. "Get your hands off me." He tightened his hold, his fingers digging into the skin of her forearm. "You're hurting me."

He loosened his grip. She stumbled backward, twisting her ankle, and a bolt of piercing pain shot from her foot to her calf. But before she made contact with the wet concrete, a pair of strong arms held her steady, and, without looking behind her, she knew the identity of her rescuer.

Jaxon.

Tom rushed to her side. "Are you okay, Katie?"

"The woman told you not to touch her," Jaxon rumbled in a deep, authoritative voice that vibrated low in her belly.

A chill unrelated to the weather spread goose bumps down her arms and pebbled her nipples into hard points. What was he doing here?

Tom puffed out his chest in a laughable attempt to compete with Jaxon for alpha male. "I don't know who the hell you are, but you'd better take your hands off my girlfriend before you regret it."

"Ex-girlfriend," she said, sliding out from Jaxon's hold and moving closer to Tom to make sure he got the message she was about to deliver. "I'll never forgive you for cheating on me with Hannah. We're through."

The snarl on his face transformed him from friend to foe. "Fine by me. Saves me having to justify to my parents why I'm wasting my time with you. Guess they were right. You can take the girl out of the trailer, but you can't take the trailer out of the girl."

A low growl was the only warning she got before Jaxon charged Tom and punched him in the nose. Tom fell to his knees, blood pouring from both nostrils. Jaxon drew back his fist for the next hit.

She caught his arm to keep him from making a mistake he'd regret. "Stop! Jaxon, it's fine. I just want to go home."

Breathing heavily, he looked like a wild man, his pupils shrunken to pinpoints and his black hair sticking up in all directions. She had to get him out of here. They couldn't afford the press or the police catching wind of him fighting. "Would you please drive me home…*Jax*?"

He lowered his fist, and his body's tension eased. He surveyed her for a moment. Then he scooped her up in his arms and carried her away, holding her to his chest. As she spotted his car on the other side of the street, she considered protesting. After all, her ankle was fine. But having him take care of her felt too damn good.

The darkness she'd expected to find in him earlier had reared its dominant head. This man wasn't the one who'd decorated the walls with paintings of rolling hills and fields of poppies.

This man had fought before.

This man believed in defending a woman's honor.

This man could be capable of murder.

Chapter Eleven

AFTER PROVIDING DIRECTIONS to her apartment, Kate melted into the heated leather seats of the car, thankful for modern technology. Shivering, she rubbed under her eyes, not surprised her fingers came away smudged with mascara.

Jaxon sat next to her, his anger almost tangible. While she looked like something between a raccoon and a drowned rat, he resembled Poseidon, powerful and dangerous. The muscles of his triceps and biceps glistened and flexed as he spun the steering wheel. She had to sit on her hands to keep herself from touching him.

So many questions bounced in her mind, she didn't know what to ask first. What was the best way to interrogate her client/pretend Dom/wannabe lover? "Do you want to tell me what happened back there?"

He ground his teeth and his muscles tensed. After a loud exhale, he said, "He hurt you."

Lots of people have hurt me. "I tripped. Accidents happen."

His lips tightened into a thin line. "That's not what I'm talking about."

Oh. *That.* Choking back the nausea, she repressed the image of Hannah riding Tom to climax and committed herself to never thinking of it again.

She pressed her hand over her heart. "I won't miss him. We were growing apart, not that we were close to start. It's the fact he cheated on me with my purported friend. I don't care I lost a boyfriend, but I will miss my friendship with Hannah."

He swore under his breath. "Good friend?"

"Best," she answered. "And the kicker? We're both interning for Nick. I have to face her every day at work knowing how little our friendship meant to her."

"You don't think you can forgive her?"

"No. Once you lie to me, I'm done. I don't give second chances."

Hannah and Tom's betrayal had transported her back to a time when she'd made the worst mistakes of her life, when her core beliefs had been shattered like a bullet to rose-colored glass.

She'd learned life's lessons the hard way. Mothers didn't always love their children. You were guilty until proven innocent. And there was no such thing as anonymity when it came to the press.

At fourteen, she'd found solace in a bottle of Jack, cocaine, and boys—many, many boys and, sometimes, grown men. When she'd climbed out of her self-imposed hell, she became determined to live in a way her father would have been proud of. Just because she no longer saw through that rose-colored glass didn't mean she had to turn cynical.

She was cautious. Which is why she'd left the past in the past and re-created a new identity without an Internet trail. No one in Detroit knew anything about her other than she'd grown up in small-town USA. She'd worked hard in college to lose her accent, although once in a while she'd slip up, especially when emotional. If someone asked about her past, she'd deflect and turn the conversation to them. Most people loved to talk about themselves.

When they reached her place, he surprised her by turning off the engine. His lips curled in disdain. "You live here?"

"I sleep here," she clarified. "I'm rarely home."

"The building should be condemned."

He wasn't wrong. The lock on the front door no longer worked, allowing anyone access. A few times she'd had to step over passed-out strangers as she climbed the stairs to her second-level apartment. The building smelled like piss and mildew and probably had black mold growing underneath the cracked tile of the entryway. But the space was rat- and roach-free, so it was good enough until she could afford both a car and an apartment in the 'burbs.

She slid out of the car, and, possibly from some misguided sense of obligation, Jaxon followed her. "If all the properties like this one were condemned in Detroit, we lower class would have nowhere to live," she said as they darted out of the rain and into her building.

He gripped her upper arm, his thumb inadvertently brushing her breast. "Don't call yourself lower class. You're a lawyer."

Tom's words still rang in her ears. *You can take the girl out of the trailer, but you can't take the trailer out of the girl.* "I'm a legal intern. No salary. After I pay tuition and books, I can hardly afford groceries." She laid her hand over his. "I live in the city because it saves gas money and the rent is cheap. It may not look like much, but it's relatively clean and the muggers say 'please' and 'thank you.'" He didn't laugh. "That was a joke."

"Not funny."

She removed his hand from her arm and pulled out her keys from her purse as she climbed the bum-free stairs to her apartment. "Not all of us can live in four-thousand-square-foot homes."

She immediately cringed, knowing she shouldn't have passed judgment on him based on his socioeconomic status. At her door, she turned to apologize. "I'm sorry. That was—"

"I wasn't always rich. I grew up a few blocks from here." He spoke quietly, the words laced with sadness.

Each moment she spent in his presence, he shattered another of her preconceived notions of Jaxon Deveroux, Dominant and high-society venture capitalist. Physically, he wasn't soft like the typical white-collared executive. No, his body was hard—harder than he could achieve with a personal trainer a couple times a week. If he'd been raised in the 'hood, he would've learned how to fight by the time he'd graduated from elementary school. You couldn't show weakness or you'd never live to adulthood.

Not only had he lived, he'd escaped poverty.

She flicked on the light, trying not to be embarrassed by her meager space, and then she realized her entire apartment could fit inside his playroom. Her living room contained an old burgundy couch she'd purchased from Goodwill and a plastic end table with a framed photo of her and her father fishing off their rowboat. The narrow galley kitchen sat behind the room and past that were the bedroom and bathroom.

Butterflies danced the jig in her belly. She dropped her purse on the couch and gripped the door handle. "Do you want to come in?"

He exhaled loudly, devouring her with his eyes. "More than anything." He crossed the threshold into her apartment. "But it's probably not a good idea."

She took his hand and led him further inside then shut the door. "You're right. It's not."

She could list dozens of reasons why making love to Jaxon would be a mistake.

He moved behind her, curling his hand around the back of her neck and squeezing.

He breathed heavily.

She couldn't breathe at all.

With the gentle pressure of his palm at the top of her spine, he rotated her until her breasts brushed the hard planes of his chest.

She raised her gaze to his face and saw everything she felt reflected there in his eyes.

Heat.

Desire.

Longing.

He slammed her against the door and crushed her mouth with his own. His lips were soft, softer than she'd imagined possible. But the kiss was not. It was a primal taking as his tongue parried and plunged, searching and exploring. Their teeth clacked together as she responded, no longer a passive participant. His taste exploded on her tongue, a mix of spicy and sweet.

A deep groan rumbled from his chest. He bent his knees, angling his pelvis to bump his erection directly against her needy bundle of nerves. She whimpered, frustrated by their wet clothing. The raging inferno licked between her legs, her pussy pulsing with spasms. Her hands drifted to his ass, his muscles clenching and flexing under her fingertips as his hips continued to grind tiny circles against her core.

He captured her wrists and tugged them high over her head, pinning her between him and the door, imprisoning her. Pleasure darted to her aching breasts. Her clit swelled and hardened, and as her panties brushed across it, her juices trickled down her thighs.

Want to touch him.

Need to touch him.

She struggled, tugging and wiggling in an attempt at escape. His grip tightened, his fingers pinching her skin.

One word pounded over and over in her head.

More. More. More.

Never in her life had she experienced passion.

Until now.

"Please," she begged, her voice raspy.

Although she wasn't sure what she was asking him for, her plea spurred him into action. He lifted her up as if she was weightless, and she wrapped her thighs around his waist. Lust crashed into her like a tidal wave, submerging her deep below the water's surface.

And she didn't want to ever come up for air.

He carried her past her couch, continuing across the living room to her bedroom, his lips hovering over hers, a whisper away.

When he stopped at the foot of her double bed, she slid down his legs to her knees. She wasn't sure if it was an accident. She didn't care. Her thighs parted and she arched her back in a submissive offering.

Not only her body.

But everything she had to give.

The significance of her gesture flashed in his eyes. She sucked her lower lip into her mouth, her teeth sinking into the soft flesh, the spice of his kiss lingering. Would he taste spicy everywhere? She reached to unbutton his pants, to give him the relief he deserved, but he caught her hand midair.

"Please," she repeated.

Her nipples pebbled from his molten gaze. He swallowed thickly and nodded once.

Craving more of his flavor, she flicked open the button of his jeans and used both hands to draw the wet fabric down his legs until he stepped out of them.

His cock sprang from its confinement, stretching proudly up to his belly from its nest of short curls. Long and thick, with a slight curve that would massage her G-spot perfectly, it twitched as she continued to admire its beauty. She'd never thought of penises as beautiful before, but there was no arguing that Jax's was a work of art deserving worship.

Cupping his heavy balls in her hand, she massaged them and kneaded them until he threw back his head with a moan, and a bead of semen dripped from the tip of his cock. She couldn't resist any longer. She ran the flat of her tongue from the base to its head, lapping up his tangy essence.

His fingers tangled in her hair, tugging just enough to bring tears to her eyes and sending a jolt of electricity to her pussy. "Suck it, Katerina," he demanded.

He may have been the Dominant, but there was no mistaking the hoarseness in his voice or the need in his eyes. She'd done this to him. She may have been the one literally on her knees, but, metaphorically, it was as if he was the one on his knees before her. Here in her bedroom, she alone had the ability to gift him with bliss.

She'd never felt so strong.

Was this an exchange of power? Or was it simply a blowjob?

Looking up at Jax as she took him deep into her mouth, she realized there was nothing simple about this man. His eyes fluttered shut when the tip of him bumped against the soft tissue of her throat. She fought the gag reflex and swallowed, breathing through her nose.

Her lips stretched around his girth, and she wrapped her hand around the base, not surprised that her thumb didn't reach her index finger. With her other hand, she cupped his testicles, rubbing her middle finger on the sensitive perineum. A couple more drops of semen coated the back of her throat and his cock jerked against the roof of her mouth. Always the perfectionist, she wouldn't stop until she engulfed him completely. Relaxing her throat muscles, she swallowed repeatedly, taking him in so deep his curls tickled her nose.

"Ah, fuck, Katerina. So good. I…you have to stop. I'm too close. It's been too long." His actions defied his words, and his legs shook as he began shallowly pumping. She slid her finger over his perineum and up the crack of his ass. "Katerina. Katerina. Katerina," he chanted breathlessly.

He cried out as, over and over, come jettisoned from his cock, and she greedily swallowed it all. High on the satisfaction of causing his strong climax, she licked her lips and grinned up at him.

From behind hooded lids, his eyes followed the movement of her tongue. He stripped off his shirt, revealing the glorious chest underneath. Between his flat, brown nipples, a light dappling of hair covered his chest, trailing to the dark curls surrounding his half-erect penis.

He fixed his hands under her arms and yanked her to her feet. As he kissed and nibbled at the sensitive spot under her ear, his nimble fingers got to work divesting her of the blouse. Desperate for his touch, her nipples poked against the fabric of her bra. He brushed his fingertips across her collarbone, so agonizingly light that if her eyes had been closed she'd swear a feather danced across her skin.

She shivered with arousal, desperately wanting to force his hand to her breast. His fingers drifted down her sternum. He spread his fingers over her small breasts and held them there.

Not. Doing. Anything.

Reminding her of who truly held the power.

The muscles inside her pussy tightened, eliciting a small whimper that tugged up his lips in satisfaction. Only then did he finally move, the rough pad of his thumb caressing her nipple through her bra, touching her as if this was the first time he'd ever touched a woman. So soft and so reverently, she could cry. She had to bite the inside of her cheek to keep from demanding more.

With a flick of his wrist, he unclasped her bra with one hand and slid the straps down her shoulders. He lowered his head to her breast and slipped a nipple into his mouth. Her hands itched to plunge into his thick hair and clasp him to her, but she sensed if she did, he'd stop.

He peered up behind his long lashes.

And bit her.

The wet folds between her thighs fluttered, and a foreign sound erupted from her throat. He soothed the bite with tiny licks and then sucked the bud into his mouth so tightly it teetered on the edge of pain. Tension built low in her belly. She was going to come, and he hadn't even touched her below the waist. Moving to her other breast, he gave it the same treatment. Her inner muscles throbbed. She ached for something to fill her. His fingers. His cock. She didn't care at this point. Whatever he wanted to give her. She'd take it. She'd die without it.

As the storm raged outside, the wind whistling and hail pummeling the windows, an even greater storm raged within. But as the orgasm began to stir, Jax stopped. Cradled her face between his hands. And stared at her as if deciding what to do next.

She whimpered, not caring if it made her seem weak. Right now she'd let him do anything he wanted to her. Anything but stop.

"Jax?" Not knowing the rules, she took one hand from her face and kissed his fingertips.

His eyes fluttered shut and he sighed. She laved the webbing between his fingers with her tongue, tasting the salt on his skin. His hands were large and his nails even, as if he'd had them manicured. But they were far from unblemished. Tiny white scars, of varying sizes, marred both sides of his hand.

His eyes shot wide open.

Dangerous.

Hungry.

Predatory.

He dropped to his knees and smoothed her slacks down over her damp thighs. Now flush with her drenched, white lace panties, he growled low in his throat, pressing a gentle kiss directly above her clit, and then he rolled her panties down her legs. His nose bumped her slit as he deeply inhaled, his grumble of appreciation easing all of her insecurities.

Using the top of his head, he propelled her to the bed, the silk of his hair like a whisper across her skin. He eased her to the edge and pressed his hands to her belly, bending her back to lie on top of the comforter and then spreading her thighs for his perusal. Her fingers curled into the blankets as she waited for him to relieve the pulsing in her pussy.

"I need to taste you, Katerina. I've been dreaming…" He didn't finish his sentence but instead swiped his tongue up one side of her labia and then the other. "You're so wet. You want this don't you? Tell me you want me."

"I do." Her hips bucked in search of his mouth. "I want you, Jax."

"Fuck," he muttered, stretching the lips of her vagina with his fingers, baring the heart of her core. "You got me, baby. You fucking got me." His tongue probed inside her tight channel, teasing her like a little cock. She arched in an attempt to take him deeper, but he restrained her with an arm over her pelvis, holding her in place.

As if she were in the last mile of a marathon, she gasped for air, a heavy pressure lodging in her chest, her heart sprinting. Sweat beaded on her forehead.

Not now, damn it. She refused to let the anxiety steal this from her. *Jax won't hurt me.*

When he pulled back the clitoral hood, exposing her tiny bud and gently flicking the tip of his tongue over it, all thought drained from her mind. The discomfort in her chest lifted, and although her heart continued to race, liquid heat flowed like lava in her belly, pressure winding into taut coils.

Murmurs of approval reverberated in Jax's throat as he lapped up the proof of her desire, driving her closer and closer to the edge of the cliff. A thick finger slipped inside, stretching her, testing her readiness. "Your pussy's like a drug. I'll never get enough."

His hair tickled her thighs as his lips descended over her sensitive bundle of nerves and sucked it between his teeth. Another finger joined the first, rubbing against a pleasurable spot high inside her channel, electrifying her. Her body shaking, the coils finally snapped, and she fell off the cliff into the ocean, overcome with wave after wave of contractions so strong, they bordered on pain.

She heard the ripping of the condom package, and then Jax was on her, sliding up her body until the head of his erect cock nudged her opening. Still shuddering with the aftershocks of her climax, she hooked her ankles around his waist and took him deep inside, reigniting the flames as if she hadn't come at all. His cock stretched her beyond comfortable, filling her. Completing her.

A round, puckered scar high on his right shoulder caught her attention. Tracing it with her finger, she silently questioned him with her eyes. Was that from a bullet?

"We all carry scars. Some are just more visible than others." Without elaborating, he dipped his head to gently kiss her, bracing his weight on his arms so he would not crush her.

A sharp sting on her shoulder tore her from her thoughts. She yelped as he bit harder into her flesh and then pinched the side of her breast until she sucked in a breath. The pain morphed into a blazing heat, and her vaginal muscles clenched around his cock.

Gliding in and out of her soaked channel, he watched for her reactions, seriousness banked in his gaze. When he bumped her cervix, she cried out, her fingers digging into the skin of his back deep enough to draw blood. He grazed her nipple with his teeth and swirled his tongue around the areola while he slipped his hand between them. Two fingers worked her swollen clit, rubbing, circling, and stroking.

Boneless, weightless, and mindless, she closed her eyes, hovering on the precipice of climax. His lips descended over hers in a bruising, claiming kiss, and his tongue plundered, mirroring the actions of his cock, driving her higher and higher.

"Come again, Katerina. Come now." He pinched her clit and bit her nipple until an explosion of light flashed behind her eyelids.

Her body bowed off the bed, and she shattered, splintering into a million pieces. This orgasm was completely different from her first, not as deep or as sharp, but equally as pleasurable.

Over and over, her pussy clamped down on his cock, and this time she watched *him* as his face contorted into a mix of pleasure-pain, eyes shut, brows furrowed, deep lines crinkling his forehead, and perspiration trailing down the side of his face.

With a shout, he shuddered, climaxing so violently she felt the pulsations inside her. She smoothed the plastered hair off his face and rained kisses down his jaw to his fluttering pulse point in his neck. He rolled off her and gathered her in his arms, staring up at the ceiling.

As a messed-up teenager, she'd fumbled with boys in the backseats of cars, the windows fogging as they groped each other with inexperienced and clumsy hands. Boys who took what she gave freely at that age, her need to feel loved by someone, anyone her only goal. Too young to know better, her body didn't soften, didn't dampen.

Then she'd had decent sex with men like Tom, which achieved mutual orgasms without dirtying the sheets or requiring a shower to clean the mix of sweat and bodily fluids from their bodies.

No question, the sex with Jax had been phenomenal. Better than when she'd placed first in her Moot Court Competition. But still, something felt…off. They'd made love. Tenderly. She'd expected sex with Jax to be the equivalent of a double-hot-fudge-cookie-dough sundae with extra whipped cream. Except for those couple of bites and pinches, their lovemaking had been closer to French vanilla.

"Jax? Can I ask you a question?" she asked.

He pressed a kiss to her forehead. "Of course. You can ask me anything."

She took a deep breath. "Did you hold back with me?"

He went completely still and a look of pain crossed his face. Then he got off the bed and started dressing.

"Jax—"

"I'm sorry. This was a mistake." His tone was flat. Lifeless.

"I don't understand. Where are you going?" She picked up a nightshirt off her floor and threw it on. "Talk to me, damn it. You owe me at least that much."

He took a step closer and reached out for her before shaking his head and dropping his hand to his side. "I'm sorry. I can't...I'm just so sorry." He turned his back on her and strode out of the room.

Completely gutted, she held back her tears and fell to her knees. Every molecule in her body screamed for her to drag him back to bed and fuck the answer out of him, but she couldn't ignore the agony in his eyes or the way his shoulders had drooped in defeat. It didn't matter how much she wanted to soothe and comfort him.

In making love with a client tonight, she'd risked her internship. Her career. *Nick*.

And for what?

Jax didn't want her. But for a few precious minutes in his arms, she'd forgotten the lesson drilled deep inside her soul at fourteen.

No one wanted her.

After all, she was a mistake.

Chapter Twelve

THE WIND HOWLED and rain pattered on the bedroom window. As a warning that she'd soon lose power, her bedroom lights flickered. Happened all the time in this rickety building.

She usually loved rainy nights.

But not tonight.

Tonight the rain reminded her of all she'd never have. All she'd lost.

Without Jaxon, her apartment seemed darker. Quieter. Colder.

If not for the delicious twinge between her thighs, she could almost convince herself she'd imagined making love with him.

But they had made love. And she wanted to do it again.

And again.

And again.

What was it about the way he'd moved inside her that made sex different with him than with previous lovers? Was that what it was like to make love to a Dominant?

Except the sex had lacked the kink she'd expected. Yes, he'd played her body like he was its master, but he hadn't demanded her obedience. Hadn't flogged or bound her.

Not that it wasn't the greatest sex of her life because it was. Her back ached from his weight on her, her nipples throbbed from his bites, and her thighs were sticky with remnants of their joining. Quite different from the sterile lovemaking she'd experienced with Tom and the drugged-out, hazy sex of her teenage years.

What had caused him to run from her? Guilt? Regret? Or was she a dud in the sack as Hannah had suggested?

Awareness slowly seeped into her consciousness. She looked at herself and realized she was on her knees, naked from the waist down. Needing a candle and lighter, she stood, her legs shaking like a newborn foal's, and opened her nightstand drawer. As she withdrew the items, her gaze fell on her vibrator, taunting her with the memory of Jaxon licking his lips when she'd told him about it.

Shivering, she ignored the sex toy and instead lit the candle and set it on her dresser.

Lightning flashed followed by an immediate boom of thunder that shook the walls of her room. Darkness flooded her apartment.

Eerie silence made her more aware of her rapid breathing.

Times like these, she wished she had a roommate. Or a really big dog.

At least she'd lit the candle before her power went out.

The first notes from Beethoven's Fifth cut through the silence and she jumped, knocking her elbow into the dresser.

Her cell phone's ring for an unknown caller.

She hesitated, her hand clenching into a tight fist against her belly as if trying to hold wild butterflies inside.

Most likely a wrong number. But what if it was Jaxon?

She lifted the candle and ambled to the couch to retrieve her phone from her purse. By the time she dug it out, she'd missed the call. She checked the display, perplexed to see her own number listed as the caller.

Her hands shook, and she dropped her phone on the carpet.

Damn it. This wasn't the first time she'd sat alone in the dark. All she needed was a panic attack to make her night complete.

She dug in her purse and flicked open her handy Tic Tac dispenser. Definitely a double kind of night. She tossed her antianxiety meds into her mouth and flinched when her phone rang again.

She snatched it from the floor and answered without checking the caller ID. "Hello?"

"Kate?" Hannah sniffed as if she'd been crying.

Anger surged to the surface. "I don't want to talk to you."

Another sniff. "Then don't talk. Just listen. I'm so sorry I hurt you. Can you ever forgive me?"

Kate sighed and massaged her temple. "No."

"Never?" Hannah's voice changed from pitiful to incredulous, as if it had never entered her mind that she'd lose their friendship over sleeping with Kate's boyfriend.

Then again, Kate had perpetuated Hannah's self-centeredness throughout the years by failing to set limits with her friend, and, like a child, Hannah had continued to test her until she'd finally crossed the line of no return. "Hannah, this isn't like the time you borrowed my favorite sweater without permission and ruined it, or the time you forgot to pick me up after class and I had to walk home in a blizzard. Those were innocent mistakes. There was nothing innocent about you and Tom."

"I didn't mean for it to happen. I love you. You're the best friend I ever had. If I could explain—"

It was as if for good measure Hannah was squeezing lemon juice on Kate's wound. "Do me a favor. Save your breath. From now on, you and I are nothing but co-workers. I hope Tom was worth our friendship. Goodbye, Hannah." She pressed *end* before her ex-friend could say another word.

Carrying her candle, she went to the kitchen and poured herself a tumbler of gin on ice, foregoing any mixer. Probably not wise to mix pills and alcohol, but since in one night she'd lost her best friend, boyfriend, and lover *and* had managed to ruin her career before it had even begun, she figured she deserved heavy sedation.

The cool liquid slid down her throat, erasing the taste of Jaxon, which lingered on her palate like the finest Belgian chocolate. With her glass in one hand and candle in the other, she flopped herself on the couch and took another sip, the gravity of tonight's actions hitting her full force.

Sex with a client.

Was she obligated to tell Nick?

Although she technically hadn't violated the rules of ethics, sleeping with Jaxon certainly wouldn't gain her a spot as an associate. Her first big case and she'd already placed the firm at risk of a lawsuit. Nick couldn't sweep this under the rug. Hadn't he warned her he'd look out for himself first? If she told him the truth, he'd have to fire her, and once word got out why she was let go from her internship, no reputable firm would ever hire her.

Even worse, she'd disappoint him. He expected more from her. Pushed her to be the best. There was no losing in Nick Trenton's world. No coming in second.

She covered her face with her hands. Jaxon wasn't only his client. He was his best friend. What if the kiss with Nick could have led to something more after graduation? She'd ruined any chance of it.

In the morning, she'd have to come clean and beg for his forgiveness. Maybe he'd take her off the case but consider keeping her on as his intern. She gulped down the last shot of gin and rolled an ice cube in her mouth. If she were in Nick's position, she'd fire her ass.

It was hopeless.

Spinning, she rested her head on the back of the couch and shut her eyes. Her arms felt as though she'd attached fifty-pound weights to them, and her breathing slowed.

Just as she slipped into unconsciousness, the trill of her phone jarred her awake. She gritted her teeth.

What would it take for Hannah to get the message?

She lifted her phone, but her fingers barely worked, making it difficult to press the green button. After several tries, she managed to connect with it. "Hannah, I mean it, don't call me—"

"Jaxon Deveroux is dangerous. You need to drop his case."

Despite the alcohol and pills suppressing her adrenaline, she jolted awake. "Who is this?"

"I can't tell you."

The caller's voice was computerized, making it impossible to identify its owner. She sat up and tried to gather her wits. Who knew her cell number? "I don't know who you think you are, but you can't accuse him of being dangerous without proof."

"You don't want proof. You want to believe he's innocent. Tell me, Katerina, did you fuck him yet?"

Bile burned her throat. Other than those she'd left behind in the Upper Peninsula, no one knew her as Katerina.

No one except Jaxon.

She coughed back her fear. "Excuse me?"

"That's what he does. He'll protect you. Convince you he'll keep you safe. Make you think you're the center of his universe and that the sun rises and sets in your cunt. But he's a sociopath. A sadist. You should know Alyssa wasn't his first."

"His first what? His first wife? Submissive?"

"His first kill. You understand what it's like to take a life, don't you, Katerina Martini? The rush. The power."

It was as if carbon monoxide replaced all the oxygen in her lungs. A stabbing pain unfurled in her chest, and she gasped for air. "I don't know what you're talking about. My name is Kate Martin."

The caller laughed. "Fine, Kate. We'll play it your way for now. It's up to you whether you choose to listen to me or not. Maybe you want to die. Maybe you think you deserve it."

A knock pounded through the door of the temporary holding cell, and a pretty female officer entered. "Katie, your mom is here."

What had taken so long? They'd locked her in here hours ago with nothing but a cup of water and some crackers. Her father's blood had dried on her clothes, and she had to pee. No way could she use the disgusting aluminum toilet in the corner.

She followed the cop upstairs to the lobby. As soon as she saw her mama, she started to cry and rushed toward her. Her head whipped back as Mama slapped her cheek.

"I never wanted a child, but I did it for him. You were a mistake. It should've been you who died in the woods."

She shook away the memory. "Don't call me again or I'll contact the police."

The caller laughed. "And tell them what? Someone warned you about your guilty client? Somehow, I don't think you'll make that call. Watch your back. Or you'll end up like Alyssa."

The call disconnected.

Spasms rocked her abdomen. Throwing her hand over her mouth, she stumbled into the bathroom, making it just in time to empty the contents of her stomach.

Her head pounded in time with her speeding heart. She rinsed out her mouth, and, as she spit into the sink, she caught sight of her weary face in the mirror. Only her swollen lips showed any evidence of her earlier bliss. Mascara circled her eyes and a line of black streaked down one cheek. Her hair stuck to her sweat-soaked head.

She could be staring at her mother's reflection.

No, she would not turn into her.

Every day people came to a crossroad and were forced to make a choice. You could give in to the darkness, admit defeat, and give up or you could travel the harder path and fight against the abyss. For a couple of years, she'd wallowed in the shadows until she'd forged a window and escaped, vowing never to return.

With the alcohol purged from her system, she dialed the only person she could trust, hoping she wouldn't live to regret it.

Don't miss the next thrilling installment of

WHITE COLLARED

BY SHELLY BELL

PART TWO: GREED

coming June 10 from Avon Red Impulse!

About the Author

SHELLY BELL writes sensual romance and erotic thrillers with high emotional stakes for her alpha heroes and kiss-ass heroines. She began writing upon the insistence of her husband, who dragged her to the store and bought her a laptop. When she's not practicing corporate law, taking care of her family, or writing, you'll find her reading the latest smutty romance.

Shelly is a member of Romance Writers of America and International Thriller Writers.

Visit her website at ShellyBellBooks.com.

Visit www.AuthorTracker.com for exclusive information on your favorite HarperCollins authors.

Give in to your impulses . . .
Read on for a sneak peek at six brand-new
e-book original tales of romance
from Avon Books.
Available now wherever e-books are sold.

CATCHING CAMERON
A Love and Football Novel
By Julie Brannagh

DARING MISS DANVERS
The Wallflower Wedding Series
By Vivienne Lorret

WOO'D IN HASTE
By Sabrina Darby

BAD GIRLS DON'T MARRY MARINES
By Codi Gary

VARIOUS STATES OF UNDRESS: CAROLINA

By Laura Simcox

WED AT LEISURE

By Sabrina Darby

An Excerpt from

CATCHING CAMERON

A Love and Football Novel

by Julie Brannagh

Sexy football player Zach Anderson and sports reporter Cameron Ondine find that their past has come back to haunt them—and maybe even ignite a few sparks—in the third installment of Julie Brannagh's irresistible new series.

Zach Anderson was in New York City again, and he wasn't happy about it. He wasn't big on crowds as a rule, except for the ones that spent Sunday afternoons six months a year cheering for him while he flattened yet another offensive lineman on his way to the guy's quarterback. He also wasn't big on having four people fussing over his hair, spraying him down with whatever it was that simulated sweat, and trying to convince him that nobody would ever know he was wearing bronzer in the resulting photos.

Then again, he was making eight figures for a national Under Armour campaign with two days' work; maybe he shouldn't bitch. The worst injury he might sustain here would be some kind of muscle pull while running away from the multiple women hanging out at the photo shoot who had already made it clear they'd be interested in spending more time with him.

He was all dolled up in UA's latest. Of course, he typically didn't wear workout clothes that were tailored and/or ironed before he pulled them on. The photo shoot was now in its second hour, and he was wondering how many damn pictures of him they actually needed. But there were worse things than being a pro football player who looked like the cover model on a workout magazine, was followed around by large numbers of hot young women, and got paid for it all.

"Gorgeous," the photographer shouted to him. "Okay, Zach. I need pensive. Thoughtful. Sensitive."

Zach shook his head briefly. "You're shitting me."

Zach's agent, Jason, shoved himself off the back wall of the room and moved into Zach's line of vision. Jason had been with him since Zach signed his first NFL contract. He was also a few years older than Zach, which came in handy. He took the long view in his professional and personal life, and encouraged Zach to do so as well.

"Come on, man. Think about the poor polar bears starving to death because they can't find enough food at the North Pole. How about the NFL jumping up to eighteen games in the regular season? If that's not enough, *Sports Illustrated's* discontinuing the swimsuit issue could make a grown man cry." Even the photographer snorted at that last one. "You can do it."

Eighteen games a season would piss Zach off more than anything else, but he gazed in the direction the photographer's assistant indicated, thought about how long it would take him to get across town to his appointment when this was over, and listened to the camera's rapid clicking once more.

"Are you sure you want to keep playing football?" the photographer called out. "The camera loves you."

"Thanks," Zach muttered. Shit. How embarrassing. If any of his four younger sisters were here right now, they'd be in hysterics.

Cameron smiled into the camera for the last time today. "Thanks for watching. I'm Cameron Ondine, and I'll see you next week on *NFL Confidential*." She waited until the floor director gave her the signal that the camera was off and stood up to stretch. Today's guest had been a twenty-five-year-old quarterback who'd just signed a five-year contract with Baltimore's team for seventy-five million dollars. Fifty million of it was guaranteed. His agent hovered just off-camera, but not close enough to prevent the guy in question from asking Cameron to accompany him to his hotel suite and "hook up."

Cameron wished she were surprised about such invitations, but they happened with depressing frequency. The network wanted her to play up what she had to offer—fresh-faced, wholesome beauty, a body she worked ninety minutes a day to maintain, and a personality that proved she wasn't just another dumb blonde. She loved her job, but she didn't love the fact that some of these guys thought sleeping with her was part of the deal her employers offered when she interviewed them.

An Excerpt from
DARING MISS DANVERS
The Wallflower Wedding Series
by Vivienne Lorret

Oliver Goswick, Viscount Rathburn, needs money, but only marriage to a proper miss will release his inheritance. There's just one solution: a mock courtship with a trusted friend.

Miss Emma Danvers knows nothing good can come of Rathburn's scheme. Still, entranced by the inexplicable hammering he causes in her heart, she agrees to play his betrothed despite her heart's warning. It's all fun and games . . . until someone falls in love!

"Shall we shake hands to seal our bargain?"

Not wanting to appear as if she lacked confidence, Emma thrust out her hand and straightened her shoulders.

Rathburn chuckled, the sound low enough and near enough that she could feel it vibrating in her ears more than she could hear it. His amused gaze teased her before it traveled down her neck, over the curve of her shoulder and down the length of her arm. He took her gloveless hand. His flesh was warm and calloused in places that made it impossible to ignore the unapologetic maleness of him.

She should have known this couldn't be a simple handshake, not with him. He wasn't like anyone else. So, why should this be any different?

He looked down at their joined hands, turning hers this way and that, seeing the contrast no doubt. His was large and tanned, his nails clean but short, leaving the very tips of his fingers exposed. Hers was small and slender, her skin creamy, her nails delicately rounded as was proper. Yet, when she looked at her hand covered by his, she felt anything but proper.

She tried to pull away, but he kept it and moved a step closer.

"I know a better way," he murmured and before she knew his intention, he tilted up her chin and bent his head.

His mouth brushed hers in a very brief kiss. So brief, in fact, she almost didn't get a sense that it had occurred at all. *Almost.*

However, she did get an impression of his lips. They were warm and softer than they appeared, but that was not to say they were soft. No, they were the perfect combination of softness while remaining firm. In addition, the flavor he left behind was intriguing. Not sweet like liquor or salty like toothpowder, but something in between, something . . . spicy. Pleasantly herbaceous, like a combination of pepper and rosemary with a mysterious flavor underneath that reminded her . . . *of the first sip of steaming chocolate on a chilly morning.* The flavor of it warmed her through. She licked her lips to be certain, but made the mistake of looking up at him.

He was staring at her lips, his brow furrowed.

The fireflies vanished from his eyes as his dark pupils expanded. The fingers that were curled beneath her chin spread out and stole around to the base of her neck. He lowered his head again, but this time he did not simply brush his lips over hers. Instead, he tasted her, flicking his tongue over the same path hers had taken.

A small, foreign sound purred in her throat. This wasn't supposed to be happening. Kissing Rathburn was wrong on so many levels. They weren't truly engaged. In fact, they were acquaintances only through her brother. They could barely stand each other. The door to the study was closed—*highly improper.* Her parents or one of the servants could walk in any minute. She should be pushing him away, not encouraging him by parting her lips and allowing his tongue entrance. She should not curl her hands over his shoulders, or discover that there was no padding in his coat. And she most definitely should not be on the verge of leaning into him—

There was a knock at the door. They split apart with a sudden jump, but the sound had come from the hall. Someone was at the front of the house.

She looked at Rathburn, watching the buttons of his waistcoat move up and down as he caught his breath. When he looked away from the door and back to her, she could see the dampness of their kiss on his lips. *Her kiss.*

He grinned and waggled his brows as if they were two criminals who'd made a lucky escape. "Not quite as buttoned-up as I thought." He licked his lips, ignoring her look of disapproval. "Mmm . . . jasmine tea. And sweet, too. I would have thought you'd prefer a more sedate China black with lemon. Then again, I never would have thought such a proper miss would have such a lush, tempting mouth either."

She pressed her lips together to blot away the remains of their kiss. "Have you no shame? It's bad enough that it happened. Must you speak of it?"

He chuckled and stroked the pad of his thumb over his bottom lip as his gaze dipped, again, to her mouth. "You're right, of course. This will have to be our secret. After all, what would happen if my grandmother discovered that beneath a façade of modesty and decorum lived a warm-blooded temptress with the taste of sweet jasmine on her lips?"

An Excerpt from
WOO'D IN HASTE
by Sabrina Darby

Miss Bianca Mansfield is ready for her
debut. If only her older sister didn't insist
on marrying first. She's doomed to wait
to find love. Until she meets . . . him.

For Lucian Dorlingsley, Viscount Asquith,
recently returned from an extended tour
abroad, it is love at first sight. He's determined
to meet Bianca, even if it means masquerading
as a tutor to her young half-brother.

A man's life can change in an instant. Lucian Dorlingsley, Viscount Asquith, heir to the Earl of Finleigh, had heard this aphorism many times, but until that particular August morning, he had never experienced such a profound moment. Not once in his sheltered childhood at his familial estate. Or during the more arduous years at Harrow and Cambridge. Not even during the long continental tour from which he had just returned.

Yet here, in the sleepy town of Watersham, where he was stopping briefly with the Colburns on his way home, his life had been rocked down to its very essence.

"I'm in love, Reggie!" He paced the length of the veranda where they were enjoying an al fresco luncheon. The sky beyond was a cerulean blue and the weather, for once, that rare balance of very English sunshine (and he had now seen enough of the world to know that sunshine had different qualities in different places) tempered by a delicate breeze. In other words, the perfect day to fall in love.

His friend, the younger brother of the Duke of Orland, looked at him doubtfully, a cautious smirk on his lips.

"Who is she, then? A Parisian dancer from the Opera? An Italian nymph? What paragon did you meet on your travels who has you so bound up in a paroxysm of amorous emotion?"

Reggie saw the world as one large jest, and on most occasions that was one of his charms. In fact, his boisterous manner was what made him so easy to be around; often Luc could simply follow him about and be amused without having to put himself forward in any way. It was also, at this moment, the one thing Luc did not need. Not about a matter so serious.

"No, nothing so cliché as all that. I saw her here, in the village this morning. I stopped by the apothecary, and there she was."

"And did you pledge your undying love to her?"

Luc shook his head, ignoring Reggie's exaggerations and persistent humor in the face of confessional honesty. An honesty that he had with few others, including his sisters. But Reggie had been the foremost companion of his youth, his roommate at Harrow and later at Cambridge. At least for the one year that Reggie had attended before he decided the pretense at study was a waste of his time. He'd been gallivanting about London ever since. "I could hardly approach her."

"I shall never understand how such a giant as yourself can be one of the most painfully shy men that I know. One would think a Grand Tour would cure you of that."

Europe had cured him, in many ways. Out of the shadow of his gregarious father, away from the judgments of his usual society, he had been able to be more himself. But now he was back in England, and . . . this was not just any woman.

"Miss Mansfield, they called her," said Luc. "Do you know her? Can she be mine?" Not that he had ever thought twice about marriage before this point. He was still young and most of his friends unattached. Yet the idea of such beauty being his . . . His own Botticelli. He looked expectantly at Reggie, but his friend's usually round, smiling face looked aghast.

"What? Is she promised to someone already? Are you in love with her, Reggie? Or is Peter? Have I lost my heart to some untouchable?"

"Untouchable, perhaps," Reggie choked out, taking a moment to twirl the long hair that fell over his forehead in sandy curls. "I didn't realize Kate was back from Brighton. But listen, Luc, this one— Forget about her. She may have been a success in London these last two seasons, but everyone in these parts knows her for the brat that she is."

Brat? Luc couldn't reconcile that word with the image that still lingered in his mind. Honey blonde hair framing a rosy-cheeked countenance. Eyes as blue as today's perfect sky. A paragon of quiet English beauty, in fact.

"She seemed quite well liked. She had a charming smile and manner. Brat seems like an unfair epithet."

"Not for Kate, but oh! Perhaps it was Bianca. Your Venus, was she fair or dark?"

An Excerpt from

BAD GIRLS DON'T MARRY MARINES

by Codi Gary

When hard-edged Valerie Willis suddenly
finds herself face-to-face with former flame
Justin Silverton, she knows her tough image
won't be enough to protect her heart.

It's been ten years since Justin kissed Val, but he's
never moved on. So when a twist of fate brings
him the chance to finally win her over during a
singles mixer, Justin's all in. Because the bad girl
who stole his heart is just too good to let go . . .

"So, why is your dad making you come down here and participate in a giant singles mixer?" Justin asked, stealing her attention away from the white slip of paper.

"He calls it good press. Guess he figures I need help finding a man," she said, wishing she hadn't answered him quite so candidly. "I don't, though. Need help, I mean."

Why are you stammering? Bending over the counter, she started filling in the blanks, hoping he couldn't see the obvious blush warming her cheeks.

"If it makes you feel any better, I never thought you needed any help in that department," he said, his voice dropping to a low whisper.

Val could feel the desk clerk's eyes on her and muttered, "Stop it."

"What? It's a compliment."

"You're just messing around to get a rise out of me."

"How is me being honest messing with you?"

"Because . . ." How did she not have a comeback to put him in his place? She always knew what to say. It was one of her strengths, but he had the ability to turn her into a stumbling, stuttering simpleton. "Because I said so."

His chuckle was a deep rumble, and her insides squeezed

in on themselves, making her cross her legs as a tingling started between them. Quickly, she handed the paper back to the desk clerk and turned to face Justin with what she hoped was a cold, hard stare.

"I don't like to be made fun of."

He seemed genuinely surprised as the desk clerk said, "Alright, Miss Willis, here is your room key and your itinerary bag. I hope you enjoy your stay in True Love and that you have a blast at the festival."

Val took the bag and key from the woman, resisting the urge to make a face. "Thank you."

Spinning away from Justin, she walked back out to her truck, only to hear him exit behind her.

"Hey!" His hand circled her arm gently, and he turned her toward him, but on the slick ground, she lost her balance. Falling against him, her face got buried in the puff of his jacket, and she wondered if the fates were trying to pull some weird *Serendipity* crap on her.

She tried to right herself, but he'd wrapped an arm around her waist and was using the other gloved hand to lift her chin, raising her gaze to meet his.

"I wasn't making fun of you. I was being serious. You're a beautiful woman. You just say the word and a dozen guys will line up to have you."

Whether it was his tone or the expression on his face, she didn't know, but her mouth suddenly seemed too dry. Words failed her, but then, who needed words when a pair of warm lips were suddenly covering hers?

As Justin kissed her, his tongue pushing past her lips, she could only hold on tight while her body turned to molten lava and the blood thundered in her ears.

Impatient honking and a loud voice yelling, "Hey, love-birds, get a room," broke through the drumbeat her heart was pounding out, and she whispered, "We shouldn't do this."

His lips touched hers lightly once more, and he whispered back, "You mean here or—"

The guy in the truck honked again and Val pulled away. "I mean, I'm not here for . . . for that."

Justin crossed his arms over his chest. "That's too bad."

Again a blast of honking ensued, and Val shot the driver a nasty look and a worse gesture before turning away from Justin and reaching for her car door. Looking over her shoulder at him, she couldn't stop herself from asking, "About the guys lined up . . ."

"Yeah?"

"I take it you're one of them?" She already knew the answer, but the small piece of her ego that had been smashed by Cole's designer shoes needed to hear it aloud.

He stepped forward and helped her into the car, grinning. "What do you think?"

She didn't answer before she closed the door and started her truck.

Why did you have to ask him that?

Because she was a glutton for torture and punishment.

An Excerpt from
VARIOUS STATES OF UNDRESS: CAROLINA

by Laura Simcox

What happens when the president's
daughter and her sexy Secret Service agent
find themselves snowbound? A little cabin
fever, some serious forbidden attraction,
and Various States of Undress . . .

Alarm coursed through Jake's blood the second his lips were on hers, but he ignored it. They'd already crossed the line, hadn't they? Hell, they'd probably crossed the line the minute they'd walked into the cabin yesterday, if he was being honest with himself. Not that he wanted to be honest right now. He just wanted more. More softness. More of her lips, which were brushing gently against his—opening, inviting.

Her fresh scent enveloped him when she wrapped her arms tighter, and he groaned, splaying his fingers across her slender back. This was wrong. No matter how safe it seemed, it would come back to haunt him. He knew that. But as his lips angled across hers and his tongue slid into her sweet mouth, the heat he found inside was intoxicating. He sank into her, returning her kisses, drawing her closer. Getting lost in her arms.

Trailing kisses across her cheeks and down her slender neck, he threaded one hand through her hair and cupped the back of her head as he bent forward, capturing her mouth again.

She let out a soft moan, and her warm hands drifted to the side of his face. She kissed him feverishly, and then her lips broke free and settled in the crook of his jaw. She whispered his name. "Jake. Jake, I want—"

"Carolina," he answered in a rush of breath. His eyes closed, and he dragged his hand from her back to caress the side of her breast. Even though she wore a couple of layers, he could tell that one of those layers wasn't a bra. His jaw tightened as he imagined her naked breasts. He wanted to taste them—and he could. Because she would let him.

Desire crashed through him, rushing straight down, making him swell in an instant. He opened his eyes and looked into hers, which were half-lidded with lust. Her head was still pillowed in his palm.

"Touch me," she said. "Please."

Instinctively, he shook his head. "I can't."

"You can." She settled her fingers over his, pushing them around her breast.

"I can," he admitted. He stared at her open mouth, aching to take it again. "But I won't."

She blinked. "We've already crossed the line, you know."

"Not completely." He let out a slow breath, lifted her back into a kneeling position, and let his hands slide away from her body.

"Far enough."

It was nowhere near far enough, but Jake couldn't think about that right now. Clearing his throat, he stood up and offered her a hand. She stared at it, not moving.

"Carolina . . ."

"Why can't we just enjoy each other?" She tilted her chin and stared up at him.

He shoved his hand into his pocket and turned away to walk into the kitchen. Once he was behind a counter, he adjusted the front of his jeans and reached for the coffee-pot. Annoyance began to seep in, killing his lust. Good. He needed the distraction of being irritated, because she *knew* the answer to her own question. He shouldn't have to spell it out.

"Why, Jake?"

He poured himself a mug and took a sip, buying time. Part of his job description was to reason with his protectees, but usually that meant explaining why, for security reasons, certain entrances, exits, and safety measures had to be used. It didn't mean reasoning with a daughter of the President of the United States . . . who wanted to sleep with him. Especially since he'd just given her every indication that he wanted the same thing.

"Your life depends on it, that's why."

An Excerpt from
WED AT LEISURE
by Sabrina Darby

In all of Sussex—scratch that—in all of England,
there is no prettier Kate than Kate Mansfield, and
Peter Colburn, heir to the Duke of Orland, has
known that since the age of 15. But since she comes
with a temper and a haughtiness to match, he's
hidden his regard behind ruthless teasing. When
his brother tries to enlist him in a campaign to
help his friend marry Kate's younger sister, Bianca,
he agrees, finally having the very excuse he needs
to approach Kate not as a combatant, but as a lover.

1810

Kate ran through the thicket, gasping, her face hot with suppressed tears. The governess would chide her for the stains and small abrasions to her dress once she returned to the house. But those admonitions were nothing compared to her mother's continued disdain.

The scent of moist earth and the sound of rushing water meant that she was close, that soon she could let go. Finally, she broke through the cluster of trees and bushes and made it to the water's edge, where she dropped down to her knees, clutched at clumps of grass with her fists, threw her head back, and wailed.

"Ahem."

Kate clamped her mouth shut and looked toward the familiar voice, embarrassment flushing her body. How humiliating.

The Earl of Bonhill sat under a tree, a book open on his lap, his trousers rolled up and his legs dangling into the stream that, a mile off, fed into the river, and that farther upstream offered her father a perfect spot for angling. The same stream that marked the boundary between the Colburns' ducal seat and the Mansfields' more modest estate. Here, however, titles hardly mattered. What did matter was that Peter had gotten there first and taken the best spot. And was now witnessing Kate in tears.

She hadn't even known he was back from Harrow.

She scrambled to her feet, glaring at him, as anger was the only possible refuge from humiliation, and headed back to the thicket.

"You don't have to run," he said, the crunch of his footsteps on the fallen leaves growing louder as he came nearer. "I'll go."

For some reason that made her more upset, and she stopped, whirling around to face him. He was 16, she knew. Four years her elder.

"It doesn't matter if you do. It's already ruined." She wouldn't be able to indulge in tears the same way anymore.

"Then maybe I can help."

"How?"

He shrugged. "Why don't you tell me why you're crying?"

"I'm not crying."

"Not anymore."

"I'm—" She shut her mouth. It wasn't worth arguing. After all, she *had* been crying.

"That's right. The fearsome Kate Mansfield makes other people cry, but she'd never be caught with such lowering emotions herself."

He was mocking her. Or needling her. Or . . .

"Just because you're an earl doesn't mean you get to be cruel."

"Someone didn't do what you want? Didn't let you have

your way?"

Frustration welled up inside her. Why was he saying such things? Of course, it was just what everyone else echoed. Everyone but her mother.

"You don't know anything about me," she said hotly, tears once again burning her eyelids.

"Then why don't you tell me?"

And for some reason she did.

About her mother, who hated her, who said she was ugly because she was so dark, who criticized everything Kate ever did, while little Bianca could do no wrong. About how no one ever paid her attention unless she did something terrible.

"So you do it on purpose, then. All the fits and tantrums we hear about—you do that for attention."

She flushed with mortification for the hundredth time that hour. She'd never thought about her reputation in the community. At twelve, her world barely existed beyond Hopford Manor. And then there was this suggestion he was making, and she wasn't certain if it was a good thing or bad. But she knew one thing, she didn't *need* attention, and his intimating that she craved it made her seem terribly weak.

"As if I'd care what anyone thinks. Especially you. Look at you. A spotted maypole!"

He flushed, which made those *spots* redden even more. There weren't all that many, but anyone would be conscious of having such flawed skin. Kate's was not. Not that one would know from the many admonishments her mother imparted about good care for one's complexion.

"You're a spoiled child, Kate Mansfield," he pronounced, picking up his book from the ground. "Maybe someday you'll grow out of it."

She watched him leave in angry frustration, hands curled into fists. It didn't matter that he was an earl and heir to a duchy, or that previously she had thought him nice and handsome and had even imagined growing up, falling in love with him, and becoming a duchess. From now on she'd stay as far away from him as possible.